"Maybe I'd better not stay,"

Chad whispered.

Being alone last night had been almost more than Veronica had been able to bear. The thought of being left alone again tonight drove shafts of panic through her. Her fingers tightened on his arms as she looked up at him. "Don't go. Please."

"If I stay…" His voice trailed off, leaving the rest unsaid.

She knew what she was asking. Knew what would happen if he remained. But she needed his comfort, needed to have him here. He understood more than anyone what she was going through. If there was a price to pay for that later, so be it. As long as she didn't have to be alone tonight.

Dear Reader,

Have you noticed our new look? Starting this month, Intimate Moments has a bigger, more mainstream design—hope you like it! And I hope you like this month's books, too, starting with Maggie Shayne's *The Brands Who Came for Christmas*. This emotional powerhouse of a tale launches Maggie's new miniseries about the Brand sisters, THE OKLAHOMA ALL-GIRL BRANDS. I hope you love it as much as I do.

A YEAR OF LOVING DANGEROUSLY continues with *Hero at Large,* a suspenseful—and passionate—tale set on the mean streets of L.A. Robyn Amos brings a master's touch to the romance of Keshon Gray and Rennie Williams. Doreen Owens Malek returns with a tale of suspense and secrets, *Made for Each Other,* and believe me…these two are! RITA Award winner Marie Ferrarella continues her popular CHILDFINDERS, INC. miniseries with *Hero for Hire,* and in January look for her CHILDFINDERS, INC. single title, *An Uncommon Hero.*

Complete the month with Maggie Price's *Dangerous Liaisons,* told with her signature grittiness and sensuality, and *Dad in Blue* by Shelley Cooper, another of the newer authors we're so proud to publish.

Then rejoin us next month as the excitement continues—right here in Intimate Moments.

Enjoy!

Leslie J. Wainger

Leslie J. Wainger
Executive Senior Editor

Please address questions and book requests to:
Silhouette Reader Service
U.S.: 3010 Walden Ave., P.O. Box 1325, Buffalo, NY 14269
Canadian: P.O. Box 609, Fort Erie, Ont. L2A 5X3

Hero for Hire
MARIE FERRARELLA

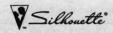

INTIMATE MOMENTS™

Published by Silhouette Books

America's Publisher of Contemporary Romance

To Tiffany & Chris,
Here's hoping
history
repeats itself

 SILHOUETTE BOOKS

ISBN 0-373-27112-3

HERO FOR HIRE

Copyright © 2000 by Marie Rydzynski-Ferrarella

All rights reserved. Except for use in any review, the reproduction
or utilization of this work in whole or in part in any form by any
electronic, mechanical or other means, now known or hereafter
invented, including xerography, photocopying and recording, or in
any information storage or retrieval system, is forbidden without
the written permission of the editorial office, Silhouette Books,
300 East 42nd Street, New York, NY 10017 U.S.A.

All characters in this book have no existence outside the imagination of
the author and have no relation whatsoever to anyone bearing the same
name or names. They are not even distantly inspired by any individual
known or unknown to the author, and all incidents are pure invention.

This edition published by arrangement with Harlequin Books S.A.

® and TM are trademarks of Harlequin Books S.A., used under license.
Trademarks indicated with ® are registered in the United States Patent
and Trademark Office, the Canadian Trade Marks Office and in other
countries.

Visit Silhouette at www.eHarlequin.com

Printed in U.S.A.

IT'S OUR 20th ANNIVERSARY!
We'll be celebrating all year,
Continuing with these fabulous titles,
On sale in November 2000.

Desire

#1327 Marriage Prey
Annette Broadrick

 #1328 Her Perfect Man
Mary Lynn Baxter

 #1329 A Cowboy's Gift
Anne McAllister

 #1330 Husband—or Enemy?
Caroline Cross

 #1331 The Virgin and the Vengeful Groom
Dixie Browning

#1332 Night Wind's Woman
Sheri WhiteFeather

Romance

 #1480 Her Honor-Bound Lawman
Karen Rose Smith

 #1481 Raffling Ryan
Kasey Michaels

#1482 The Millionaire's Waitress Wife
Carolyn Zane

 #1483 The Doctor's Medicine Woman
Donna Clayton

#1484 The Third Kiss
Leanna Wilson

#1485 The Wedding Lullaby
Melissa McClone

Special Edition

 **#1357 A Man Alone**
Lindsay McKenna

 **#1358 The Rancher Next Door**
Susan Mallery

#1359 Sophie's Scandal
Penny Richards

#1360 The Bridal Quest
Jennifer Mikels

 #1361 Baby of Convenience
Diana Whitney

#1362 Just Eight Months Old...
Tori Carrington

Intimate Moments

 #1039 The Brands Who Came for Christmas
Maggie Shayne

 #1040 Hero at Large
Robyn Amos

#1041 Made for Each Other
Doreen Owens Malek

 #1042 Hero for Hire
Marie Ferrarella

#1043 Dangerous Liaisons
Maggie Price

#1044 Dad in Blue
Shelley Cooper

Chapter 1

He saw the pain in her eyes the moment she walked into his office.

Another man not in his line of work would have noticed the young woman's slender figure, the honey-blond hair smartly done up in a variation of a French twist with just a few rebellious hairs out of place at her temples, or the cut of her clothes. She was wearing a powder-blue, single-breasted jacket and skirt that most definitely hadn't come off some department-store rack fingered by the general public. This woman, with her hundred-dollar-an-ounce perfume that softly entered the room with her, was someone of taste and breeding who knew exactly what was becoming to her and who could easily afford it, no matter what the price.

All those things registered, but only on a secondary level. Because the pain in her eyes captured the bulk of Chad Andreini's attention and immediately expressed to him the fact that a life-and-death situation had brought her here.

He half rose in his chair, fragments of manners his mother had once tried to teach him before she wasn't able to teach him anything anymore surfacing automatically. Politeness, she had liked to say, never went out of style. He hoped, in the world his mother now inhabited, that it never did.

The woman entering his office seemed oblivious to the courtly gesture. It was apparent that she was fighting for composure as she moved toward him. She was employing that strange, disembodied gait that people find themselves unconsciously resorting to when their entire worlds are crumbling down around them and they can't understand why they are still drawing breath, still alive, when something very precious has been snatched from them. Perhaps forever, though the thought was always far too horrible to contemplate.

She had that look about her.

He'd seen it before and would see it again, but it was nothing he would ever get used to.

Carrie, the secretary he and the others at ChildFinders, Inc. all used, had buzzed him half a minute earlier, telling him that a new client was here. It was his turn to try to pick up the pieces of this latest case and glue them into some semblance of a whole as he attempted to solve the puzzle. He knew nothing more about her than her name. Veronica Lancaster.

She looked like a Veronica, he thought now, silently taking measure of her. The woman's bearing was regal. Regal even in the time of a parent's worst nightmare.

At least, that was the facade.

But Chad knew how easily and quickly facades could crack and break apart, letting everything within spill out. Leaving only an empty vessel and a fading memory of composure in its wake.

Veronica Lancaster, for all her effort, looked close to breaking apart.

He liked to keep his distance. It helped keep his mind clear and focused on what was important. Right now, he felt like a spectator at a pending disaster. The feeling left him wanting to do something to prevent it. It was not only his job to do something about it, it was his calling.

"Please sit down, Mrs. Lancaster."

Veronica heard the gently worded instruction. The voice was deep, strong. It penetrated the constantly recurring fog about her brain, and she looked around the room, focusing for the first time. There was a chair right in front of his desk.

Veronica complied with the man's urging. It didn't occur to her not to.

Hands on the chair's arms, she lowered herself into it slowly, as if some part of her was afraid that any sudden movement might make her collapse into it.

Or collapse entirely.

Oh Casey....baby...how could this have happened? she thought.

Veronica felt moisture beginning to form at the corners of her eyes and she blinked as she drew air into her lungs. The silly thought came to her that if she filled herself completely with air this way, it would prevent anything from spilling out that wasn't supposed to.

Like the wail of agony that scratched and clawed at her throat, threatening to burst out.

She couldn't break apart, she couldn't, she ordered herself silently. She had to hold herself together. Every second counted. Every moment she gave way to despair and the abject terror that was tightening around her heart was a moment she couldn't use, a moment that was taken away from rectifying this incredible, horrible wrong that had been done.

A moment that might mean the difference between Casey's coming home and not.

Taking another breath, she began, "My baby..."

No, he wasn't a baby. Casey hadn't been a baby for quite some time. He liked to draw himself up importantly and crisply informed her of that fact whenever she slipped and called him that.

I'm not your baby, Mama.

But he was. He would always be her baby. And someone had stolen her baby.

And her world.

''My son, Casey,'' she corrected herself with effort, ''has been kidnapped.''

Chad Andreini nodded his head slowly, encouragingly, as if what she had just said was a revelation and not the obvious reason anyone would come to the agency in the first place.

ChildFinders, Inc., specialized in recovering kidnapped children and in locating runaways. It had originally been established when Cade Townsend's own son, Darin, had been kidnapped. The agency had a record of success rivaled by none. Recovering kidnapped children was a cause very dear to Chad's own heart, having been one himself once. There had been no terror involved in his kidnapping, other than the lie that had been tendered to him as the truth—that his mother, younger brother and sister had all been killed in a car accident. No terror and no suspicion because the man telling the lie had been his own father. His father, who had abducted him from his home so cleverly that no one had suspected a thing.

It would probably have continued to remain a secret for a long time, instead of just two years had Chad not, in a fit of youthful rebellion, left his father's house and hitchhiked back to his old neighborhood. It had come in the wake of yet another argument with his father, and Chad had been determined to return to a time and place when life had been less traumatic for him.

The trauma had come, anyway. Seeing his mother, barely functioning in her grief over losing

him, and his brother and sister alive had been a
shock. But it paled in comparison to the fierce sting
of betrayal he felt when he realized that the man he
had placed at the center of his universe, had kidnapped him from life as he knew it and lied to him.

It was something he frequently buried in his
mind, but never managed to quite get over, even
after his father had been sent to prison.

Odd how things worked. That event in his far-
away past had brought him to this place in time,
sitting at this desk. Waiting to listen to this woman
with the pain-filled green eyes.

Eyes that were fighting back tears.

In a fluid motion, Chad reached over to the small,
state-of-the-art tape recorder beside his computer
and pressed the record button. The second he did,
he saw apprehension bloom in her face.

Her eyes darted to the small sleek machine.
"What are you doing?"

"Recording this meeting." Did she have something to hide? He studied her quietly, toying with
half-formed notions.

Distaste entered her eyes as she continued looking at the recorder. Veronica Lancaster had grown
up living a fish-bowl existence where microphones
and cameras were periodically pointed at her for
one reason or another through no fault of her own.
Her great-great-grandfather had assured the family
fortune through methods that had not always wel-
comed scrutiny in the light of day. It took three

generations and sizable contributions to almost every major charity for that to be smoothed over.

Now all that was remembered was that there had been a couple named Lancaster on the *Mayflower,* newly married young travelers who had made that first crossing to a brave new world almost four hundred years ago.

It seemed to Veronica that people were always interested in what the Lancasters were doing, treating them as if they were a cross between their next-door neighbors and visiting gods. Veronica had grown up hungering for privacy the way a person on a never-ending diet hungered for a taste of chocolate.

Knuckles taut and white, she struggled to keep her voice from quavering as she nodded at the tape recorder. "Is that really necessary?"

Chad made no effort to turn the machine off. His yes was silent.

"It helps us piece things together. You might forget things later," he told her, his voice low, quiet. "Sometimes things you've overlooked come back to you when you listen." The machine remained on, softly whirling. There were few rules at the agency, other than Don't Fail, but Cade insisted on having the first interview with a client recorded. Chad saw no reason to break that rule. But he saw that having the recorder on troubled his client. He understood the desire for privacy, too. "Pretend it's not there."

The half smile, tinged in irony, rose to her lips

unconsciously. Easier said than done, she thought. "I've spent half my life pretending it wasn't there."

Light-brown brows drew together over the bridge of Chad's nose. "Excuse me?"

She raised her eyes to his. Veronica knew she sounded as if she was babbling. Her mind felt so scattered, so out of focus. She couldn't seem to catch hold of a single thought for more than a moment.

Was it possible he didn't know who she was? Maybe. Right now, she wasn't certain who she was herself. Other than a mother whose heart had just been ripped out. When she'd first realized what had happened, it had been a struggle just keeping herself together and breathing. Every fiber of her being had wanted to cry out for help.

But who was there to call? Just acquaintances. And family members who were on the fringe of her existence. Not even her own family, but Robert's.

Robert was gone and he had been the only one she had ever permitted herself to lean on. So there had been no one to turn to, no one to call.

Just as well. The voice on the phone had warned her not to call anyone. Not to tell anyone that Casey had been kidnapped.

Or else...

Or else. The two most horrible words she had ever heard. Veronica couldn't bring herself to finish the sentence, not even in her mind. The consequences were too terrible for her to contemplate.

"Nothing," she murmured, dismissing her rambling comment.

Talk, damn it, Ronnie. You're wasting precious time.

"I went to pick up my son this afternoon and he wasn't there." This time the tears did break through, trickling from the corners of her eyes. Angry with herself, she quickly wiped them away with the side of her hand. "I'm sorry," she murmured. "I'm not like this normally."

Coming around the front of the desk, Chad handed her a tissue. "There's nothing normal about this." Gently he prodded her along. "Where were you picking your son up from?"

Veronica drew what composure she could manage back to her, covering herself in the remaining shreds. It was hard to think.

"A birthday party. Andy Sullivan's fifth birthday party. The Sullivans don't live far from us and..." Her voice broke. Why hadn't she remained with him? Why had she left Casey and gone? Other parents had stayed. Defending herself from her own accusations, she raised her head and looked at Chad. "I didn't want to be one of those overprotective mothers. I didn't want him being afraid of his own shadow, the way—"

Abruptly she broke off, waving away the rest of her words. The investigator looking at her with intense blue eyes didn't need to know about the fears that had been inflicted on her by a feelingless nanny to whom her grandfather had arbitrarily handed over the responsibility of raising his two orphaned grandchildren—her and her sister, Stephanie. That had no bearing on this.

Nothing had a bearing, except finding Casey.

Struggling, she continued. "I went to pick him up and he wasn't there. Anne—"

"Anne?" Looking at her, he jotted the name down on the small pad before him.

She was getting ahead of herself again, tripping over her thoughts as they ran up at her from all directions at once. It wasn't going to do Casey any good if she kept falling apart like this.

Veronica tried again. "Anne Sullivan, Andy's mother. Anne said she hadn't seen Casey since the cake was served. The children were playing different games…"

He nodded, encouraging her. "How many children would you say were at the party?" He saw the bewildered look in her eyes. She was focusing on her son; the others didn't exist for her. "Take a guess. Five? Ten?"

She shrugged helplessly before she could stop the gesture. "Thirty, forty—Anne Sullivan knows a lot of people."

With that many around, it was simple enough to lose track of one small boy for a few minutes. And he knew that a few minutes was all it took. "Was the birthday party being held at the house?"

Questions, he was asking her questions when all she wanted him to do was run out and find Casey. Now. Bring him back to her before anything…

She was behaving like a madwoman, like someone she didn't even know.

Biting her lower lip, Veronica forced herself to focus. She nodded. "Outside. On the grounds. There were other parents there, and Anne had clowns..."

Strangers working their way easily amid the children. It got harder. "Maybe..."

She knew what he was thinking before he said it and shook her head. "Casey hates clowns. He would never have gone off with one of them. Not without screaming."

This investigator, Chad Andreini, sounded so calm, she thought, as if they were discussing a movie they'd both seen, instead of something that was ripping her apart with sharp, lethal talons. She was desperate to have this all said and out of the way so that this somber-faced man leaning back against the desk in front of her would make it right somehow. She would give him anything he wanted, as long as he would make it right. As long as he would bring Casey back to her. Nothing meant anything without Casey.

Chad made a notation to check out the clowns, anyway. He stopped writing when Veronica continued in a faltering voice.

"Anne started to help me look for Casey and then the housekeeper came out to say there was a phone call for me."

As he waited, she paused as if to gather together courage to face the rest of the words she had to say.

The phone call that turned vague uneasiness into a stark, frightening reality.

"The voice on the other end said that he had Casey. That if I told the police or anyone else, even Anne, about this, I'd never see Casey again. He said that Casey was safe and that he wouldn't be harmed if I did exactly as I was told. And then he said he would be in touch later with instructions." Anger and loathing filled her voice. "He told me to be 'a good girl' and then the line went dead."

"Did you recognize...?"

Again she shook her head, this time adamantly. Did he think she'd be coming to a stranger for help if she'd had the slightest suspicion about who had kidnapped her son?

"No. I'm not even sure if it was a man or a woman talking." She saw the way he raised his brow. He probably thought she was losing her mind. Maybe she was. "The voice was tinny—metallic, like something you'd hear coming out of a robot. It didn't even sound human."

The kidnapper was using a synthesizer. Which could mean that she might be able to recognize the voice under ordinary circumstances, Chad thought. Or not. His habit was not to let any one thought lead him off until he'd heard everything.

"What did you tell Mrs. Sullivan when you hung up?"

Veronica shrugged vaguely. "The first thing that came into my head. That Casey's uncle had come by and picked him up without telling anyone. That he was the one on the phone, calling to let me know.'' Her eyes asked him if she'd done the right thing. ''I—I didn't want to take any chances.''

He nodded. The woman could think clearly in a crisis. He wondered how clearly. The next question that came to him came from his own past experience. ''Are you and your husband together?''

Startled by the query, Veronica stared at him in silence for a second before answering. ''No.''

Chad's father had stolen him in the aftermath of what had been an ugly custody battle. His father had been denied access to his family except for a handful of holidays, and even those, Chad had later discovered, were to be under supervision. History had a nasty habit of repeating itself. ''Do you have any reason to believe that your husband would take your son?''

Veronica closed her eyes, pushing away the fresh onslaught of pain. She felt like a mouse, running from corner to corner, trying to elude a cat hot on its scent and bent on swallowing it whole. She hated this feeling, hated this helplessness she was trying to conquer.

Her voice was hollow when she answered. ''My husband is dead, Mr. Andreini. He died in a plane crash almost eighteen months ago. I'm a widow.''

And she hadn't come to terms with that yet, he thought. A kernel of sympathy pushed forward. ''I'm sorry.''

The words, tendered politely, still had a devastating effect on the emotional fences Veronica was desperately attempting to keep up. The last of her composure shattered.

"I don't need you to be sorry, Mr. Andreini," she snapped at him. "I need you to be good at your job. I need you to find my son for me before... before..."

Embarrassed by her behavior, Veronica swallowed a curse at her own frailty and at him for bringing it out. "I'm sorry. I shouldn't be taking this out on you."

"No need to be sorry, Mrs. Lancaster. I understand."

She wished he wasn't being kind to her. Right now she didn't need someone being kind; she needed someone snapping at her, making her angry. Making her cope. Kindness was dissolving her resolve.

"It's Ms. Lancaster," she corrected him. "Lancaster's my family name. Robert said it sounded better than his—Reinholt. He joked that maybe someday he'd change his name to mine. He was very progressive that way..."

Talking about her husband drove her over the edge of endurance. The next thing she knew, she was breaking down completely and sobbing, unable to stop.

At a loss, Chad looked at the closed door and thought of calling his sister into the office. Megan was so much better at this kind of thing than he was. She knew how to be sympathetic while he had no idea how to handle a woman's tears. It wasn't in his nature. Even Rusty, his brother, who had come into the firm just before he'd joined it himself was better at dealing with this than Chad was. Rusty was warm, engaging and outgoing.

Hell, they were all better at this than he was, probably even the janitor.

But they weren't here in the room with this woman, and he was. And her sobs were tearing at his heart. He thought of leaving, of getting someone, but that was the coward's way out and too close to abandonment, however fleeting, to suit him.

Awkwardly he took hold of her shoulders and raised Veronica to her feet. She didn't seem to be aware that he was doing it. But the moment he did, she collapsed against him, burying her face in his chest and sobbing uncontrollably.

Chad had no choice but to stand there and hold her. And silently make her a promise. He was going to find her son no matter what it took.

Chapter 2

The scent of unfamiliar cologne nudged its way into the depths of her grief, pulling her back up to the surface. She straightened again, determined to get control of herself. Raising her head, Veronica looked up at the stranger whose arms she had just been in. Embarrassment washed over her.

He was probably used to this kind of behavior, she thought. But she wasn't used to behaving this way and it shamed her. "I'm sorry, I don't know what came over me," she said.

She'd been raised not to show emotion, he guessed. Or maybe she'd learned along the way not to in order to survive. He could understand that. It gave them something in common. What little comfort he could offer, he did.

"You're scared and you just gave in to every single bad thought that's hammering away at you, trying to break in."

And, he added silently, she had every right to be scared. Any intelligent person would be. There were a lot of variables at play here. A lot of ways this could end unacceptably. But she didn't need to hear any of them. She needed to hear something to buoy her spirits, something to hang on to. That was part of his job, too, even if it was a part that didn't come naturally to him the way it did to Megan and Rusty.

His eyes met hers. He had silently given her his pledge. He fully intended to make good on it.

"I am here to tell you that you're going to get your son back, Ms. Lancaster. You have my word on it."

"Thank you." The two small words had her entire heart behind them.

The look on her face pinned him to his promise as surely as a monarch butterfly being pinned to a bulletin board.

Chad turned away and fished out another tissue from the box on his desk. Pressing it into her hand, he waited until she wiped her eyes.

He watched Veronica as she bunched the tissue in the palm of her hand and then threw it away. He got back to his questions. "Did the kidnapper tell you when to expect the call?"

She shook her head. The investigator was probably wondering what she was doing here when the kidnapper could be calling at any moment. She indicated her purse.

"I have call-forwarding. If he calls while I'm here, it'll come through on my cell phone."

Sitting home, waiting without having set any wheels in motion for Casey's recovery, would have driven her crazy. She blessed the whim of fate that had sent her to her dentist's office with a toothache last month. It was there that she'd overheard a conversation about a kidnapping with a happy ending that had brought her to ChildFinders.

Call-forwarding. She was thinking—a good sign, Chad thought. He glanced at the tape recorder. There were still a great many questions he had to ask her. Invasive, personal questions designed to enable him to get a better picture of who Veronica Lancaster was and why this had happened. Why her child and not someone else's, if, in reality, she had actually been singled out. He wondered how she was going to bear up.

The agency dealt with every sort of missing-child scenario. Kidnapping cases fell under a variety of headings, this one being the kind that attracted the most attention, piquing the interest of news reporters. A child held for ransom rather than snatched by a social deviate or taken to fill an emotional hole left by a child who had been lost or perhaps never even conceived. The stuff headlines were made of.

A kidnapping for money meant, at the very least, that the kidnapper was in some way familiar with his chosen target, with the family's lifestyle, as well

as their comings and goings. That it might be someone that Veronica was at least slightly acquainted
with might make this case easier.

Or more difficult, he thought, depending on the
circumstances.

It was his experience that familiar surroundings
helped clients. ''There're still a great many questions I have to ask you,'' he said. ''Would you be
more comfortable at home?''

''I'm not going to be comfortable anywhere, Mr.
Andreini, until I get Casey safely back.''

He nodded. ''I understand.''

The way he said it, she had the impression that
he actually did. But how could he? How could he
know what it felt like, having a son just snatched
away? There one moment, gone the next without a
trace. She bit her lower lip to keep from accusing
him of being patronizing. He was trying to be nice.
But she didn't want *nice,* she wanted results. Now.
Before she lost her mind.

''But I still do have more questions to ask you,
Ms. Lancaster,'' he was saying. ''You might feel
better answering them at home. And seeing Casey's
room might give me a better sense of your son.''

She didn't want to go home. Didn't want to walk
in and know that Casey wasn't going to be there
somewhere, bedeviling Angela, her housekeeper,
with his antics, winning a free and clear pardon
with nothing more than his infectious laugh and a
smile that lit up a room.

But he was right, this tall, solemn-eyed blond

detective. She should be home. And if there was something there that helped him find Casey even a minute sooner, then it was worth the agony she knew she was going to go through.

With a nod of her head, Veronica began steeling herself for the ordeal.

The emptiness assaulted her the second she closed the door behind her. She'd never thought she'd go through anything worse than having Robert die. She was wrong. Though every part of her tried feverishly to hang on to the hope that Casey would be home soon, fear was attempting to beat her down into a deep, slick-walled pit of despair.

Turning when she didn't follow him, Chad saw the look in her eyes. Knew the dangerous state her mind was in. Instinct had him taking her hand, as if the physical act could pull her out.

"We'll get him back," Chad said again, this time with more feeling than he generally employed. "You have to believe that. We are going to get him back, and whoever took him is going to pay."

"I'm not interested in revenge."

"Then you're a rare woman, indeed, Ms. Lancaster. But the kidnapper is playing a dangerous game and he has to be made to pay for it." He squeezed her hand, surprising himself with the intimate action. He usually stood on the perimeter, gathering information and doing what he was paid to do. "It'll be all right," he promised. "Now, why don't you show me Casey's room?"

With a single nod of her head, she led the way up the stairs. Without thinking, Veronica left her hand in his. It helped.

The door to Casey's room was open. Facing west, it received the afternoon sun, which was even now spilling out into the hall. It gave the room a warmth Chad instinctively knew was part and parcel of the boy.

He took a step inside and looked around slowly. It wasn't a huge room, but there was a great deal to take in.

Veronica hung back in the doorway, warning herself not to cry again. She'd done all the self-indulging she intended to do. Her eyes came to rest on the drawings on his bulletin board.

"He's just a normal little boy."

A smile in reaction to her words played on Chad's lips despite the gravity of the situation. There was a regular computer, not a child's version of one, on one side of the room. Stacked around it in neat piles were boxes of educational software. A fifteen-inch television set was directly across from it. The set was hooked up to, not one, but two different gaming units, one on each side. In between were hip-level bookcases with either books, games or action figures occupying every available space.

For all its paraphernalia, he had to admit that the room was the neatest child's room he'd ever seen.

"Not hardly," he commented under his breath. "It looks like a toy store exploded in here."

It was a valid observation. Veronica lifted one

shoulder in a shrug. "I suppose I've spoiled him a little since his father died, but Casey doesn't take anything for granted," she said proudly. "I was more self-centered as a child than Casey is. There was as much joy in his eyes when he got a new action figure as when I gave him that game set." She indicated the one closest to Chad.

He'd taken note of that one first. It was all the rage these days, according to Rusty. His younger brother had the heart of a boy and kept him abreast of what was in and what wasn't. The gaming unit was definitely the hot item of the moment.

"I never have anything to complain about with Casey. I couldn't have asked for a better son than if I'd ordered him directly from heaven." Veronica found herself before the bulletin board, staring at the drawing he'd done just the other day. It was of the two of them. She had gangly legs and wayward curls, courtesy of a yellow crayon. She was holding what passed for flowers in her elongated hands. Like the flowers Casey had picked for her out of the garden, much to the gardener's dismay. Veronica's eyes filled with tears again. Blinking them back, she turned away before she trusted herself to look up at Chad again. "In a way, I guess I did."

Was the boy adopted? That brought in a complete set of new possibilities if he was. A natural mother, suffering the pangs of delayed regret, could have taken Veronica's son. The ransom aspect might be a ruse. "Come again?"

It wasn't something she talked about, but if this

man was going to find Casey, maybe he needed to know all the details. At least he needed to know how precious the boy was to her.

Taking out the thumbtack, she held the drawing to her chest. "It took me a long time to get pregnant with Casey. Five years." Looking back, it seemed a great deal longer than that. "There were endless tests, exploratory surgery…" Her voice trailed off. Everything she'd been subjected to faded the instant she'd held her baby in her arms for the first time.

A fresh volley of panic shot through her. Veronica gripped Chad's arm. "I can't lose him now. I'll give you anything you want—"

He cut her short. She had to understand that for him, for all of them at the agency, it wasn't about money. "Standard rates, Ms. Lancaster. I put in the same amount of effort—one hundred and ten percent—into finding a lost child whether there's a family crest or not."

She would have traded in every last cent if it meant that Casey would never have had to go through this. It was because of who he was, who *she* was, that he'd been kidnapped. Children from poor families didn't get kidnapped for ransoms.

Veronica shook her head. "No family crest." A hint of a bittersweet smile whispered faintly across her lips. "My grandfather would probably roll over in his grave if he could hear me saying this, but that ancestor who came over on the *Mayflower* was an indentured servant just one voyage ahead of a hangman's noose. He and his wife both were."

Chad nodded as he took in the information. At least she wasn't a snob. "The common touch."

"Very common."

It remained to be seen, Chad mused, if their kidnapper fell into that category.

He took his time looking through Casey's things, trying to get a sense of the boy. He talked to Veronica as he worked. For all intents and purposes, Casey seemed like a child with above-average intelligence, a happy-go-lucky kid with eclectic taste. The action figures, arranged in a scene of combat, looked as well used as the second game set did.

What caught Chad's attention was a framed photograph on the far end of the bookcase of Veronica on her knees, holding her son to her. He examined it, trying to envision the scene that had been taking place when the photograph was taken. They were both laughing. Veronica looked radiant.

Someone had taken her child and extinguished that light.

Veronica came up behind him. Despite the raft of photographs she had from professional sittings, the one Chad was holding was her favorite of the two of them.

"That was taken the first day of kindergarten." She could vividly remember every detail. Casey had been torn between wanting to run off to the new adventure and wanting to remain behind with her. She'd encouraged the former and loved him dearly for the latter. "This past September," she added for clarity.

There was a building in the background. Chad peered more closely at the photograph, trying to make out the name. It seemed vaguely familiar, and he assumed that he had passed it on one occasion or another. "What school does Casey attend?"

"Los Naranjos."

The name clicked. Chad looked at her. "That's a public school."

"Yes, I know. That's part of keeping Casey grounded and not letting him get a swelled head about who he is."

Had that been a mistake? she wondered suddenly. Was it someone she'd encountered at the school who had planned this awful thing? Would Casey have been safer if she had sent him to a private school, where the screening process was exacting and the security was tight?

"Do you know anyone who might want to take him? Have you seen someone hanging around lately? Have you received any threatening phone calls in the last month or so? Any strange calls at all, people hanging up, that sort of thing?" Chad asked.

To each question Veronica shook her head, feeling more and more agitated. She looked at the tape recorder Chad had placed on Casey's computer desk. The soft whirring noise was almost undetectable, especially compared to the racing of her heart. But she hated it. She'd assumed since he hadn't instructed her to talk into it or near it that it could pick up sounds from all over the room. Like an

invasive intruder. Like the intruder who had come
into her world.

In an effort to gather her nerves, she took a deep
breath, then let it out. "As far as I can tell, I don't
have any enemies, Mr. Andreini. There's nobody
who would want to do this to me." She felt a flash
of temper. "Don't you think if there had been I
would have reported it to the police or gotten a
bodyguard?"

Hindsight, he thought. Veronica Lancaster was
upbraiding herself for not having it.

"It doesn't necessarily have to be an enemy,"
he said. He studied her face for a sign as he asked,
"No disgruntled boyfriend trying to get even?"

"No. I don't have time for boyfriends, Mr. Andreini."

Chad resumed going through Casey's things.
"Chad," he corrected without looking at her.

He hated being called Mr. Andreini. It made him
think of his father. There'd been a time when he
had toyed with the idea of changing his last name,
severing all ties with the man who had upended his
life so brutally. But in the end, because Megan and
Rusty had made no effort to change their surname,
Chad had dropped the idea. The name tied him
more to them than to his father.

"How about your husband's parents?" Turning,
he looked at her again. "Are they still alive?"

There'd been a card at Christmas. And a generous check in lieu of a gift, which would have required time and effort on their parts. But she bore

the couple no malice. It was their loss. She'd deposited the check into the account she'd started for Casey with the money from Robert's life insurance.

"They live in Europe, Mr.—" she corrected herself "—Chad, and are frankly far more interested in their three poodles than in their only grandchild."

She was trying hard not to show it, but he'd caught a hint of bitterness in her voice. Undoubtedly on Casey's behalf. "Your husband was an only child?"

"He has a brother—" She stopped abruptly. She wasn't some soft-brained person to be led from question to question without understanding the direction. "Where are you going with this?" she wanted to know. Surely he couldn't be thinking of accusing Neil. Casey's uncle wasn't exactly an eager beaver when it came to doing anything meaningful with his life, but he adored the boy. "Neil dotes on him. Some monster did this." She began to sound more like herself to her own ear. Confident. In control. "I don't know any monsters, Chad. Can't you get that through your head?"

She was loyal, protective. All good qualities. But at times they tended to make a person blind. He'd learned not to instantly rule out anything on faith. He had to be convinced. Still, he wasn't about to waste time arguing, either, other than to say, "Well, some monster apparently knows you, Veronica."

Veronica opened her mouth to respond but never got the chance.

Chad was about to suggest that she take him to the site of the party—Anne Sullivan's house. He wanted to find out what agencies the woman had employed to supply the food and the entertainment, as well as the names of any regular household help she had. From where he stood, he was looking at all the earmarks of an inside job. This had not been a random kidnapping, but one that had been planned. Someone knew something, and it was up to him to follow whatever trails there were until he came to a scrap of information he could use. It was a little like being a rat following different paths in a maze. One of the paths had to lead to something substantial.

But before he could make the suggestion, a high-pitched, urgent ring came from the purse she was still holding.

Veronica stared down at her purse dumbly for a moment, as if the sound rendered her incapable of thought. And then the words "The kidnapper!" burst from her lips. She had forgotten to cancel call-forwarding when they'd walked into the house.

"Answer it," Chad instructed quietly.

The urging snapped her back to the world of the functioning. Wrapping her thoughts around a fragment of a prayer, she quickly took out the cell phone, snapping back the lid as she did so. Chad motioned for her to tilt it slightly so that he could hear.

Her heart was pounding so hard she could barely breathe.

"Hello?"

A high-pitched whine preceded the first word. "Took your sweet time answering. I was beginning to think maybe you'd changed your mind about the boy and didn't care if you got him back."

She wanted to scream at the person on the other end, to demand the reason he was doing this to her. To Casey. It was everything she could do to keep her voice level. The only thing she could ever remember her father saying to her was never negotiate from a position of fear. The other side could always smell fear.

So she did her best to sound annoyed at the suggestion. "Yes, I want him back. I want him back very much."

The laugh, metallic, discordant, went right through her. "I'm counting on it."

Her eyes met Chad's. She could feel her breathing begin to regulate. Having him here helped her cope. "What is it you want?"

"What do you think?" The sneer transcended the metallic sound.

Her father's edict began to fade. "I'll give you anything you want, just don't hurt him."

"Hey," the voice said carelessly. "If he gets hurt, it won't be my fault."

A fresh wave of fear assaulted her. Holding the phone in both hands, she angled it closer to her. "What do you mean?"

Very gently Chad moved the cell phone so that they could both hear it again.

The voice on the other end said, "You're a smart lady. You figure it out."

"Please, no games, just tell me how much you want and where to bring it." She disregarded the expression on Chad's face as he shook his head.

The voice laughed again. "Oh, but I like games, Ronnie. I really do—"

The line suddenly went dead.

"Hello? Hello?" she cried frantically, her voice going up. There was no response. "Damn it, answer me!" Veronica shouted into the telephone.

Chad took the cell phone from her, placing it to his own ear. The line remained dead.

The eyes that met his were bordering on frantic. "I charged it—it can't be dead."

"It's not the phone's fault." Chad flipped it closed again and then handed it back to her. "In all probability, he's just playing with you."

"Playing with me?" she echoed in stunned disbelief. "Why? Why would he do something like that?" This was about money, wasn't it? She'd already established to her own satisfaction that it wasn't anyone out for revenge at some slight.

"To accomplish just what he's done," Chad said. "To keep you off balance so you don't start thinking and piecing things together. Things he doesn't want you to piece together."

"Like what?" she demanded.

"That's what we're going to have to find out." He took out his own cell phone and began punching in numbers.

She was so frustrated she could scream. Panicking when she saw him take out his phone, Veronica placed her hand on the keypad. "What are you doing? You're not calling the police, are you?"

In his estimation, having the police around, except perhaps for a chosen few individuals, was not advisable at the moment. He'd seen too much on the force he'd left behind to be blindly trusting.

"No, I'm playing a hunch." He drew the phone away from her. "It's what you're paying me for," he reminded her gently. The phone on the other end rang three times. Sam Walters, he knew, was away on a case. But his wife wasn't. A soft voice filled his ear. "Savannah? Chad. I need a little information." He thought he heard the sound of laughter in the background. That would be Savannah's girls, he thought. Two very live wires who rarely slept. He didn't know how the woman did it. "Can I get you to look up something for me on your computer?"

"If I can," Savannah replied. "What is it you need?"

He saw Veronica looking at him, undoubtedly trying to second-guess his request. "See if there've been any power outages or downed phone lines anywhere between here and L.A. County and Riverside."

Savannah's soft laugh filled his ear. "Don't ask for much, do you?"

"Never more than you can deliver. Call me on my cell when you find out."

"Will do. New case?"

Savannah had come into Sam's life when he had set out to find her missing daughter. She knew first-hand what a mother in this situation felt like. He could have used her earlier in his office when Veronica had broken down.

"Yes."

"Tell your clients they couldn't be in better hands. Good luck, Chad."

He smiled. "Thanks." Breaking the connection, he flipped the cover shut on his phone.

Veronica watched him put away his phone. She didn't realize she was holding her breath until she spoke again and found that her lungs ached. "Now what?"

"Now I continue asking you questions."

She wanted to be doing something. Hitting something. "But the kidnapper..."

He'd seen all he needed to in the boy's room. Gently he escorted her out into the hallway. "He'll call again. And we'll be waiting for him."

The operative word, she knew, was *waiting*. She didn't know if she was going to be able to much longer.

Chapter 3

"Who calls you Ronnie?"

Veronica stopped at the head of the stairs and turned to look at Chad uncomprehendingly. "What?"

"The voice on the other end of the line called you Ronnie." He didn't see her as a Ronnie. Ronnies were dark-haired women who excelled in competitive sports and laughed out loud when something tickled their funny bone. The woman before him looked far too sophisticated to manage more than a small smile. "Who calls you Ronnie?" he repeated.

Her response was immediate. "Nobody." And then she stopped, backtracking. Remembering. "Robert did. And sometimes I do—in my mind when I'm frustrated," she added. "But nobody else does." That wasn't altogether true. "Except for Stephanie," she amended. "That's my younger sister. She was the first one to call me that when she couldn't wrap her tongue around 'Veronica.'" That seemed so long ago now, she thought. She found herself wishing her sister was here, instead of on the other side of the country.

She hadn't mentioned a sister before. Getting information in dribs and drabs was not something he was unaccustomed to. "And where is your younger sister?"

Veronica could feel herself growing defensive. "In New York. She's a curator at the Museum of Natural History. And not a candidate for suspicion." He was wasting time looking in directions that led to dead ends.

He could almost read the thoughts crossing her mind. "I'm just trying to get a clear picture, that's all, Veronica."

She was vaguely aware that he'd stopped addressing her formally. "The picture is crystal clear. Someone, not my sister, not my brother-in-law, but someone," she emphasized, "came to Andy Sullivan's birthday party and walked off with my son."

According to her, there had been a great many people at the party. Still, children that age did tend to shy away from people they didn't know. "Would he go off with a stranger that easily?"

Feeling suddenly weak, Veronica leaned against the wall. She ran a hand over her pounding forehead, but the throbbing continued. The headache was nearly blinding. She should have been stricter with Casey, should have made him more wary of people.

She could feel the sting of gathering tears again and willed them back.

"I wish I could say no, but other than a phobia of clowns, Casey is the world's friendliest kid. I've tried to tell him over and over again not to talk to strangers, but…" Helpless, she tried to ward off the feeling with a shrug.

That one simple gesture transformed her from a regal queen into someone who embodied vulnerability and frailty. Chad felt something distant stir within him, prompting responses that were nearly foreign to him. It made him want to comfort her.

The best comfort she could possibly have would be the recovery of her son. He pushed on. "And there's no one else who calls you Ronnie?"

Fighting her headache, she straightened again. "No, why? Is it important?"

He shrugged noncommittally. "Might have narrowed the playing field a little. 'Veronica' is rather a formal name while 'Ronnie' is on a different, more intimate level."

She gave a laugh, short and without humor. "Which is a polite way of saying that 'Veronica' sounds like a snob."

Memories from her past, cruel ones with taunting children who took painful shyness for aloofness and used insults and gibes to make themselves feel better, surfaced. She pushed them aside. This wasn't the time for that, or for feeling sorry for herself.

She rarely felt sorry for herself. Hadn't felt the inclination since Robert had died. Now the emotion waited for a moment of weakness to suck her in.

"My word would have been 'regal,'" Chad told her easily. "'Ronnie' sounds familiar. As if who-ever's on the line knows you."

The idea was completely foreign to her, com-pletely unacceptable. When she finally spoke, her voice was hollow. "I don't know anyone who would do something like this. It's not hard to get money from me, Mr.—Chad. I'm a soft touch."

Soft wouldn't be the first word he'd think of, looking at her. But it had definitely suggested itself in the first few minutes.

He studied her for a moment. "Are you?"

"Yes." She thought of Robert. The few times they'd had words, it was over her largesse, her ten-dency to be taken in by every sad story, not so much because she believed it word for word, but because she hated seeing people worried over money matters. Money was there to ease suffering, not be the cause of it. Robert disagreed. "So much so that my husband took over the finances when we were married. He said that otherwise, I would sin-gle-handedly get rid of money in a decade that took three generations of Lancasters to accumulate." She dismissed her generosity of spirit with a single disparaging sentence. "I'm a sucker for any sob story."

He sincerely doubted if the dictionary definition of the word was applicable to her. "Funny, I wouldn't have pegged you as a sucker."

This time her laugh was softer. She raised her eyes to his, surprised he could make a kind assessment. He looked very hard to her. As if nonsense was something he hadn't even a nodding acquaintance with. "Which just goes to show that appearances are deceiving."

His point exactly. "Right. I want you to remember that."

She felt like someone who'd fallen into a trap without seeing any of the telltale signs. "Meaning?"

"Meaning that someone around you might have decided that a handout wasn't enough. They realized that they now want the whole hand." He studied her face, watching for any giveaway. "Know anyone like that?"

That same defensive feeling rose again, higher this time. She refused to believe what he was telling her. Veronica had spent years building up her confidence, convincing herself that there were people who wanted things from her other than just her money. That they were satisfied with her company.

She raised her chin defiantly, her eyes daring him to prove her wrong. "No."

She was lying, he thought, and wondered why. Was she reluctant to reveal something to him because he was an outsider? It wouldn't be the first time. Hiring a private investigator was a mixed bag.

You were asking a stranger for help in exchange for money. Along with that money, you were being forced to bare your soul, something that didn't come easily to most people. Certainly not in times of crisis.

Chad took no offense. He was accustomed to being on the outside. It had become his personal niche over the years, standing on the far side of everything. It made him an observer. And good at his job.

He pushed a little. "I'm on your side, Veronica," he reminded her. "If there's someone you think you're protecting…"

"Why in heaven's name would I hire you and then try to protect someone?"

It wasn't so farfetched. Megan had had a case where the kidnapper had turned out to be the ex-husband. His wife, their client, had gone on defending him to the end. Chad fixed Veronica with a long look. "I don't know. That's for you to tell me."

"I'm not. Protecting anyone," she added after a beat. "You have to believe me, nothing and no one means as much to me as my little boy." Veronica waved her hand around the well-lit hall with its collection of paintings that could easily have been housed in a museum. "I'd give up everything in a blink of an eye to have him back unharmed. As for protecting anyone…"

Veronica stopped for a moment. She pressed her lips together, debating. Her eyes slid over the pho-

tograph she still held in her hand. The one that
Chad was going to have copied to show to people.
Casey's photograph. The scale tipped.

There was fresh resolve in her eyes when she
looked up at him. "I know several people with
cash-flow problems and one person who is being
blackmailed."

Blackmail. Someone being blackmailed could
turn desperate. Discreetly pressing the record button
on the tape recorder in his jacket pocket, he took
out a pencil and began to write on a fresh page in
his notepad. "I'm going to need names."

Second thoughts sprang up. She didn't want to
put anyone through more than they were already
enduring. "None of them would take Casey. They
wouldn't have to. I'm a very loyal friend, Chad."
If she had it, she'd give it. The word no was not in
her vocabulary when it came to money.

"I've no doubt you are." Somewhere in the back
of his mind, he entertained the thought that it might
be nice to have a friend like Veronica in his corner.
If he was ever in a position to need friends. Which
he wasn't. His job required a certain amount of net-
working, but that was apart from the concept of
friends. He even kept his distance from Sam and
Cade, as well as Megan and Rusty, although he was
as close to them as he was to anyone. "Your loyalty
isn't in question here, but as a rule, people can do
some very ugly things when they find their back
pressed to the wall. Ugly things even they wouldn't
dream themselves capable of." She was wavering.

He could see it. "Let's start with the blackmailing victim."

Veronica sighed, giving up the name. "Erica Saunders."

He wrote it down. "Does Erica know who's blackmailing her?"

Veronica shook her head. "It's being done over the computer."

Chad shook his head. "Ah, the benefits of technology." He'd settle for an old-fashioned typewriter any day. He looked down at Veronica. "What is she being blackmailed for?"

She hesitated, but knew it was useless to keep silent. She'd already given up Erica's name. "She had a fling with someone on a vacation she took."

So far, that didn't sound like anything to try to hide. There had to be more to the story. "And?"

Veronica felt as if she was betraying a trust. She looked away. "And she has a jealous husband. A very jealous older husband. At first she could manage the money, but now..." She spread her hands wide, imitating a gesture Erica had used when she finally broke down in her living room and told her story.

"And she came to you."

"No, actually I went to her. I dropped by and found her with a gun in her hand. Her husband's gun." Veronica looked at Chad, leaving the rest unsaid. "She told me because she knew I wouldn't tell anyone."

And now that she was, it was eating away at her,

he thought. But there were more important things at stake than Veronica's conscience. "Think of me as a priest. And remember Casey."

Did he think she needed to be reminded? "I can't think of anything else." She looked around him at the telephone in the hallway. There were phones in all the rooms. Silent phones. "Don't you think they should be calling back by now?" She could feel herself beginning to battle hysteria again. "How long does it take to get to a telephone?"

If downed lines had prompted the abrupt disconnection, that depended on how wide the affected area was. "Maybe the grid failure is widespread. Not everyone has a cell phone." He saw her look at hers. "And even if they do, they'd be fools to use it."

"Why?"

"Highly traceable." He got back to the list. So far, there was only one name on it. She'd made it sound as if there were more. "Anybody else putting the touch on you? You mentioned several people with cash-flow problems."

This time the hesitation was longer. He could see that her nerves were getting the better of her again, chewing away at her fragile hold on sanity as she stared at the telephone.

"My brother-in-law," she finally said.

Since she didn't elaborate, he made a guess. "Sister's husband?"

She looked at him, realizing that she'd momentarily drifted off. She had to keep focused. "No,

Robert's younger brother.'' She saw a look come into Chad's eyes. He obviously suspected Neil again. ''He made some investments. They're not doing too well now...'' At least, that was the story he'd given her when he'd asked her for a ''loan.'' But he was family, and she could no more turn him away than she could dance on the moon. ''He has a trust fund, but he can't access enough to—''

''Trust fund?'' As far as he knew, trust funds were for children. ''Just how old is your brother-in-law?''

''Twenty-five. No, he just turned twenty-six.'' Not that the extra year had brought any extra wisdom to Neil. He was one of those people forever destined to be a boy trapped in a man's body. ''His father didn't feel that he was capable of handling the money he inherited from his grandmother sensibly.'' Robert had shared that opinion, she recalled.

''Father knows best,'' Chad murmured, turning a page and continuing to make more notes.

As soon as the words were out of his mouth, it struck him how utterly ironic the phrase was, coming from him. In his case, father hadn't known best. Father had known only how to inflict torment on all those around him. And on some who were far away.

He returned to the empty space above the information. ''What did you say your brother-in-law's name was?''

''Neil. Neil Reinholt.''

The name was vaguely familiar. Something about

an overnight stay in jail and a party that had gotten out of hand. He made a mental note to do a great deal of checking into Reinholt's past. "Anyone else?"

There were a few more minor loans here and there, but nothing on the level she'd given Erica and Neil. She shook her head. "Nothing of consequence."

"I'll be the judge of that." When the cell phone rang, she nearly jumped out of her skin. He placed his hand on her arm automatically, as if that could somehow calm her down and reassure her. "That's mine, not yours." Hand still on her arm, he dug into his pocket and pulled out his phone. With a snap of his wrist, he flipped the cover open. "Andreini."

"Are you anywhere near a television set?"

It was Savannah. The lady was quick. He glanced toward Casey's room. "Close enough, why?"

"Flip on any channel," she told him. "The story's all over the news. They're cutting into the local programming to make the announcement." She saved him the trouble of having to watch. Sam had told her how much Chad hated to have things dragged out. "A truck swerved and catapulted off the 405 freeway overpass into some telephone lines. Lines are down through Newport Beach, Bedford and parts of Santa Ana and Tustin. They're not sure how long it's going to take to have them up and running again."

Newport Beach, Tustin, Bedford and Santa Ana. That encompassed a pretty sizable area.

Turning on his heel as Veronica watched, Chad made his way back to Casey's room and switched on the television set. The next moment, an earnest-looking young Asian-American woman dressed in a mint-green suit came on, her words captured mid-sentence as she went over the details of what Savannah had just told him.

"...and there's no telling just how long this will continue. Local crews are out en masse, trying to rectify the damage. Stay tuned to Channel Six news for up-to-the-minute coverage of this story..."

He'd heard all he needed to know. "Thanks, Savannah."

"Anytime. Anything else?"

He looked down at the notepad he was still holding. "As a matter of fact—" Flipping back the page, Chad glanced at the names he'd written down. "—I want you to see what you might come up with on an Erica Saunders." He saw Veronica's eyes widen and then annoyance enter as she placed her hand over the pad.

"Emergency or faster?" Savannah was asking.

He drew the pad away from Veronica. "The latter." He shoved the pad into his jacket pocket for the moment. "You're the best."

He heard her laugh on the other end. "So I keep reminding Sam."

"If he can't remember that on his own, I'll remind him for you."

"It's a deal. Call you when I have something."

"Thanks." Chad flipped his cell phone cover down, then tucked the phone back into his pocket. He read the wariness in Veronica's eyes. "We're all discreet at ChildFinders, Veronica. Mrs. Saunders's husband isn't going to find out a thing—and we might."

It was asking too much for her to believe that her best friend had had Casey kidnapped. Erica was his godmother, for heaven's sake. "I refuse to believe that Erica could be capable of—"

He cut her short. "No offense, Veronica, but you would be surprised what your friend might be capable of." His gaze pinned her. "What even you might be capable of, under the right circumstances. Anyone looking at you would say you were too delicate to kill someone."

She thought of the shiver that had gone through her just touching the gun that Erica had held in her hands. "What are you—?"

"But in the right situation," he continued as if he hadn't heard her protest, "say, defending your son, you might be capable of just that."

She knew he was right. To keep Casey safe, she would do anything, including kill someone. "Why are you trying to deliberately shake me up?"

It wasn't to see that look in her eyes, although it did make her appear wildly vibrant, instead of gracefully refined. "Because I need you to be aware of things, Veronica. And I want you to tell me the truth. About everything,'' he stressed. ''No holding back for whatever reason. This is a puzzle...''

A puzzle? Did he take this to be just another game to challenge himself with? A game with a fat check as a prize at the end? ''This is my son's life,'' she said to him hotly.

Chad's voice remained calm. ''This is a puzzle,'' he repeated, trying to make his point, ''in which even the smallest piece might trigger us to see the larger whole. I want and need every small piece you can get your hands on, so to speak. It's important,'' he said, his eyes never leaving hers. ''We'll just sit here and go over everything you can think of—until the phone rings again,'' he added, knowing that was foremost in her mind.

She swallowed and found that her throat was completely dry. Veronica put her fears into words. ''And if it doesn't ring?''

No chance of that happening, he thought. ''You're lucky, Veronica. The kidnapper is not after your son as a keepsake. Casey hasn't been selected because someone is trying to line their pockets by selling kids, or because some mentally unbalanced person thinks he's her son brought back to life. Whoever took Casey just wants your money. The phone'll ring,'' he assured her with conviction that came from instinct and years of training.

He looked at the room they had already left once. This wasn't the best place to conduct the rest of his questioning, he thought. Just being here pained her.

It would be best if he got her downstairs on more neutral territory.

He indicated the hallway. "I'd love a cup of coffee."

Training returned to her. Veronica pressed her lips together and nodded. "Angela's gone for the day, but I think I can manage a cup of coffee." She turned toward the doorway.

He followed immediately behind her. "Angela?"

"My housekeeper."

There'd been no one in the house when they arrived. He assumed that the housekeeper didn't live in. That would make it easier for the woman if she was behind this. "How long has she been with you?"

"Since I married Robert. Ten years," Veronica added when she realized Chad was still waiting for a number.

He stopped at the bottom of the landing to jot down the woman's connection. "What's her last name?"

"Evans." She watched him write it down. "You can't possibly suspect Angela."

Chad fixed her with a long, studying look. "Yes," he replied quietly, "I can. I can suspect anyone. I'm a very distrusting person, Veronica. It's what makes me good at what I do."

She saw the merit in that, but knew how it could interfere with the rest of his life. "How do you turn that off?"

The answer was short, succinct. "I don't."

For the first time she looked at him as something other than an investigator. "Doesn't that make things difficult for you?"

He smiled, knowing where she was going with her question. "I don't dabble in those kind of things," he answered. "My work keeps me very busy. There isn't time for anything else."

She'd heard that excuse before. It was one she'd given herself. Before Robert had come along.

Chapter 4

Her heart leaped to her throat when she heard the ringing sound again just as she reached the bottom of the stairs. It had her grabbing for her cell phone even though the ring was different from her own. Hope made her irrational.

"It's mine again," Chad told her, slipping out his phone and opening it. It was too soon for Savannah to be getting back to him, he thought. Even Savannah wasn't this fast.

The call was from Rusty and had nothing to do with the business at hand. Chad could tell by his brother's unusually subdued voice that something was not right with the universe. His younger brother was ordinarily one of those people who needed no excuse to be genuinely happy. His exuberance was missing.

''Chad, do you have any free time tonight?''

Chad glanced at Veronica before answering. He intended to wait with her until the call came through from the kidnapper. There was no way of gauging how long that would be. Under normal circumstances, he would finish asking his questions and then return to the office where he'd begin a methodical investigation. But the kidnapper's aborted call, whether intentional and merely aided and abetted by the power failure, or accidental, had left Veronica hanging. He wasn't about to walk away from her until she heard the actual demand.

Turning away, he lowered his voice. ''I don't know yet. Why, what's up?''

''I'm not sure,'' Rusty replied. ''But I don't think you want me to talk about it on the phone. Give me a call when you're available.''

Chad's curiosity was mildly aroused. There were no real question marks in his personal day-to-day existence. His life was spartan-like. Outside of his cases, he had very little going on. He got together occasionally with his brother and sister, and even less often with the other three men in the firm, Cade Townsend, Sam Walters and Ben Underwood.

It wasn't that he was antisocial; he was just self-contained. His job was to reunite parents with their children. He had no place in that sphere once his work was done, and now three of his partners, including Megan, had life partners of their own. He didn't fit in.

''You okay?'' he asked. He knew that when it

came to himself, Rusty never liked to complain. Which was why when he'd had appendicitis, they had barely gotten him to the hospital in time.

There was a slight hesitation, followed quickly by an overcompensated assurance. "Me? Oh yeah, I'm fine."

Chad took it at face value. "Then I'll call you when I can." With that, Chad flipped his cell phone closed.

She was looking at him with hungry eyes, hoping for a scrap. "Was that about—?"

He cut her off before she continued to work herself up. "No, that was a personal call."

The tight-lipped way he said it told Veronica that was as much information as she was going to get on the subject. It wasn't that she wanted to pry into his affairs. It was just that she was desperate for a distraction, any distraction, until the kidnapper finally got back to her. But the phone in her hand remained silent. She looked at it accusingly.

"About that coffee," he prodded gently, taking her elbow.

The words made her snap back into her surroundings. "Right. Coffee."

Veronica looked vaguely toward the rear of the house. She was seriously beginning to doubt she remembered how to make coffee. Or how to find her way to the kitchen.

She managed both.

Moving woodenly, she pulled out two cups, one for him and one for herself. When the coffee was

finally ready, she poured them with a hand she was
struggling to keep from shaking. Taking a seat opposite Chad at the kitchen table, she held on to her
cup with both hands as if she secretly hoped it was
a way of channeling the kidnapper, forcing him to
make the call.

But nothing rang. She sincerely hoped that the
downed phone lines were not making the kidnapper
angry. What if he took that anger out on Casey?

What if...?

She forced herself not to go there. Not to think.
Instead, she stared into her china cup, watching
how the overhead light skimmed along the inky surface of her untouched coffee.

"Have you been at this long?" She tried to make
herself sound as if she was interested in the response, but her voice sounded dull to her own ear.

Chad leaned back in his chair. He tried to remember if he'd ever seen anyone with skin paler
than hers. She looked as if the slightest thing would
set her off. He debated asking if there were any
mild tranquilizers in her medicine cabinet she could
take. His mother's medicine cabinet had always
been full of them. Different prescriptions from different doctors all with the same mission: to make
her forget her pain.

Chad decided, for the time being, not to ask. Still
studying her, he set down his cup. "Investigation
in general or recovering lost children?"

Lost. The word echoed back at her, mocking her.
Lost. As if she'd misplaced Casey somewhere like

a sweater that had been absently shed. Casey wasn't lost—he was stolen.

She lifted one shoulder, then let it drop. The smile was minimal, but genuine as her eyes met his. "Take your pick. I probably won't remember what you say, anyway," she added in a flash of bare honesty.

He liked the lack of pretense. There was nothing he valued more than honesty. And nothing, he knew, that was rarer. Chad took a long sip before answering. The coffee could have been better. He doubted anyone ever complimented Veronica Lancaster on her coffee-making skills.

"I was on the police force for five years." He paused, taking another sip. "Being with Child-Finders suits me better. It's a focus."

The word hit her wrong, snapping her tenuous hold on overly frayed nerves. "That's all it is to you? A focus?"

She had a right to rail. He took no offense. She was going through hell. If shouting at him helped her, it was all part of the job. "A very good, rewarding focus. We have an amazing success record. It's an unbroken streak."

"Yes, I know." Her mouth was so dry she could hardly get the words out. What was wrong with her? Why couldn't she remain in control for more than a few minutes at a time? "I'm sorry, I didn't mean to…"

He waved away the apology. There was no need

to compound her frustration with embarrassment. "That's okay."

She nodded her thanks, then sighed as she set down the untouched cup. "You know what they say about streaks."

Yes, he knew what they said. That streaks ended. It was inevitable. Everything ended eventually. But she needed hope, not reality, with its pessimistic bent.

Chad placed his hand on her wrist, drawing her eyes to his. "This one won't end here." He needed to get her mind occupied. "Can you give me a list of people who were at the party?"

She blew out a breath, struggling to lift the fog from her brain. "A partial one."

He turned his pad to a clean page. "Go ahead." She gave him six names, then hit a wall. "No problem," he assured her. "I can get the rest from Mrs. Sullivan."

Terror leaped into her eyes. He couldn't say anything to arouse suspicion. Common sense warred with fear. "He said not to tell anyone."

"He meant anyone official. Police, FBI. That's all kidnappers ever worry about." He saw she was unconvinced. "We can start out by telling your friend that you want to hire the same caterers and entertainers for a party for Casey." That had a drawback. "But if she knows your son dislikes clowns…"

Veronica nodded, understanding. "Do whatever you think is best. Just get me my son back."

He made a couple of more notes to himself, ideas that had just occurred to him. "That goes without saying."

"But I want you to keep saying it. Keep saying it until he's here." Maybe if she kept repeating it, if he kept repeating it, then it would happen.

She realized that she'd reverted back to one of her old childish beliefs. If you believed hard enough in something, it would happen.

"I'm sorry. You probably feel like you're baby-sitting an overgrown child."

"Nothing to apologize for. You're going through hell and you need to believe that heaven's waiting for you."

That was one way to put it, she thought.

The doorbell rang, cutting off her breath. On her feet so quickly that she upset both her coffee cup and her chair, Veronica left both where they fell. She ran to the front door with Chad only half a step behind her.

He knew what she was thinking. That somehow Casey had eluded his kidnapper and found his way back home. Hadn't that been what had actually happened with him? The only difference was that he hadn't known it at the time. He hadn't realized that he was leaving his kidnapper behind. All he'd known was that he'd walked out on his father when the man had been too drunk to realize what was happening.

But cases like his were not common. This kidnapping was entirely different from his own. There was no mentally unbalanced ex-husband in the wings waiting for his chance.

The motive was ransom, he reminded himself, pure and simple.

Except that there was never anything pure or simple about kidnapping.

Chad reached the door ahead of her, his legs being longer. She looked at him in surprise when he placed his hand over the doorknob. "I'll take it from here," he told her. Just in case.

Hand near the weapon he always carried on his person, Chad opened the door. He saw a casually dressed, dark-haired man of medium build slouching more than standing on the doorstep. Beside the man was a woman who looked far too flashy for him. She was half a head taller than he was, wearing jeans and a tight aqua sweater, and his hand around her waist.

The man's expression turned from openly genial to confused as he looked up at Chad, who was a good five inches taller.

A very faint whiff of alcohol floated in. The man peered through the doorway. "Veronica?"

Veronica squeezed in beside Chad, her body brushing his as she forced the door farther open. Her tension telegraphed itself to Chad in the single contact. She was looking at the man. "Neil, this isn't a good time."

Confusion changed to a not-too-subtle smirk as pale blue eyes took in both of them one at a time. Neil held one hand up in silent protest at his error.

"Hey, sorry, I didn't mean to interrupt anything." He turned to look at the woman beside him. "C'mon, Jo, we can come back tomorrow."

Torn, Veronica debated between asking her brother-in-law in and telling him everything or just letting him go on his way. But Neil's companion temporarily took the decision away from her.

The well-endowed woman's deep-brown eyes slid over Chad with unabashed interest. Her appraisal of him was obviously favorable, for she gently pushed Neil across the threshold and into the house. She never took her eyes off Chad.

Her smile bordered on wicked as she inclined her head toward Veronica, her eyes still fixed on him. "Who's your friend, Veronica?"

For a moment Veronica's mind went completely blank. But before Chad could say anything, she managed to recover. "You're not the only one with a social life, Josephine." Her voice became stronger as she slipped further into the lie. "Chad, this is my brother-in-law, Neil, and his girlfriend, Josephine."

If the preamble to her introduction surprised him, Chad gave no indication. Instead, he extended his hand to first Neil, then Josephine. He kept his interest in them covert.

His assessment was rapid and thorough. Neil gave every indication that he drank too much and enjoyed it even more. His companion looked like a hundred other women Chad had come across during his career. Women who aged too quickly and whose fire went out too fast. Women who traded on what they had before it was gone, hoping to upgrade their lives.

"Chad, huh?" Josephine's eyes drifted over him again. She seemed to like what she saw a little more each time. "Nice name. Nice bod, too." But even as she said it, Josephine tucked both her arms through Neil's and hung on, beaming. There was no doubt in Chad's mind that Josephine regarded Neil as her trophy.

And that Neil was eating it up.

"You've got to excuse Jo—she likes to speak her mind." Neil laughed, patting the hands that rested on his arm. He winked at Chad. "What there is of it." He glanced at his companion. "Don't talk too much, Jo. You don't want to use yourself up."

Josephine's only response was a high-pitched giggle better suited to a character in a Saturday-morning cartoon program.

Normally Veronica enjoyed Neil's company. He made her laugh and, except for one instance, was like the younger brother she'd never had. With Stephanie in New York, Neil was her only family, besides Casey.

But right now, she wasn't up to Neil's antics and certainly not to Josephine's.

"Did you come here for a specific reason, Neil?" Impatience prompted Veronica's question. "Because if you didn't…"

The dark head bobbed up and down. "I understand. Here." He thrust a small bag at her. "I promised Casey I'd pick this up for him the next time I went to Dodger Stadium.'' The grin was just the slightest bit sloppy, testifying to his imbibing more than one beer at the stadium. ''It's an autographed baseball from...''

Veronica took out the plastic-encased ball. She read the almost illegible signature. It was Casey's favorite pitcher. *Oh Casey, I wish I could just run up to your room and give this to you.*

''Is he around?'' Neil asked, walking farther in. He looked up the staircase. ''I'd kind of like to see his face when he sees what I got him.''

Clutching the gift, Veronica turned around. She started to say that Casey was still at the party, but the words never made it to her lips. Instead, she began to cry.

When Josephine looked at him quizzically, Chad moved forward and slipped his arm around Veronica, pretending to comfort her, keeping up the ruse that Veronica had started. Josephine looked properly placated and just a shade envious.

Flustered, Neil looked from Chad to Veronica. ''Hey, it's only a baseball.'' The pleased look on his face turned to a distraught helplessness. ''This wasn't something that Bobby talked about giving Casey, was it? Because if he did, you know I don't pay attention to that kind of stuff. Just goes in one ear and out the other.'' He dragged a hand through his unruly hair, apparently stymied as to how to rectify the situation. ''I didn't mean to stir up any memories for you, Veronica, honest.''

Trying to regain her composure, Veronica held her hand up to stop him. She shook her head, only marginally aware that Chad had slipped his arm around her in mute comfort. She was behaving like a fool and she hated it. "No, it's just that…"

Lies were only going to complicate things. Thinking fast, Chad decided that someone had to know the truth. Besides, he wanted to see Neil's reaction.

"Casey's been abducted." He watched each of their faces as Neil and Josephine absorbed the terse sentence. Disbelief and shock registered on Neil's, while Josephine appeared as if she was having trouble assimilating the information. He could almost see her struggling with the words.

Josephine cocked her head, auburn hair spilling over her bare shoulder. "Abducted. Does that mean he's been—"

"Kidnapped," Neil snapped at her, sobering instantly. "How dumb are you?" Ignoring Josephine, as well as Chad, he took Veronica's hands into his own. "When? How?"

"Today, from the birthday party I took him to."

Neil looked as if he was having trouble breathing. His grasp tightened on her hands. "Are you sure?"

For all the world, she wished she could say no. "Yes."

Neil's eyes darted back and forth between Veronica and the tall stranger standing beside her. He looked as if he didn't trust Chad. "How much does the kidnapper want?'' he asked Veronica. Before she could answer, he added, ''Can you raise it?''

Because he could see how much it distressed her to talk about it, Chad answered for her. ''The amount wasn't specified. The connection broke off before she could find out.''

Neil turned to Chad. ''Have you called the police yet?''

''No police,'' Veronica said quickly to squelch any ideas he might have of calling them himself. ''He said he'd kill Casey if I called anyone.''

Hanging on the fringes of the conversation, Josephine moved forward. ''So what *are* you going to do?''

Drawing on what felt like her last reserve of inner strength, Veronica squared her shoulders. She would not fall apart again, she swore to herself. She couldn't afford to. She glanced at Chad before answering. ''We're going to wait.''

The answer didn't sit well with Neil, but it was her call. He shoved his hands deep into his pockets in muted frustration. ''Want us to…?''

Anticipating his offer, Veronica rejected it as gently as possible. Having them here waiting with her would only increase her agitation. She was in no mood for anyone's company—especially his girlfriend's, the latest entry in a long parade of airheads Neil had hooked up with since he'd first reached puberty.

''No, that's all right, Neil. Really.'' She began

urging him toward the door. ''I appreciate the offer, but I'm better off alone.''

Josephine followed without any coaxing. ''Doesn't look as if you're alone from where I'm standing.'' She made no effort to hide her smirk as she gave Chad another long appraising look.

Neil looked somewhat annoyed as he took hold of Josephine's arm and pulled her after him through the front door.

''Okay, we'll leave,'' he told Veronica. And then his expression softened. ''But if there's anything you want, Veronica, anything you need, just call.''

Touched, Veronica leaned over and kissed him lightly on the cheek, knowing he was sincere, if sadly ineffectual. Neil looked enough like Robert to have been his twin, but the similarity between the two brothers ended on the surface. Neil had never possessed any of Robert's ambition or his backbone. The only thing the two had in common when it came to personalities was that both were good men in their own way.

''I know, Neil.'' Veronica took a step back. ''Thank you.''

He placed a hand against the door, keeping her from closing it. ''Call me if you hear anything. Okay?''

She nodded, praying she would have something to tell him soon. ''I will, I promise.''

Still, Neil stood wavering in the doorway, wrestling with his thoughts and a conscience he rarely heeded even as Josephine was tugging on his arm to leave. His last words were directed at Chad. "Look, you're new to me so I don't know just how serious things are between you and Veronica. But she's the best, so be good to her or, as puny as I look in comparison to you, I'll find a way to break every bone in your body. Okay?"

The threat didn't bring the expected smile to Chad's lips. "Okay," Chad promised with a sincerity that pretense and undercover work had long since made easy for him.

Chad closed the door behind Neil and Josephine. Flipping the lock and testing it, he turned around to look at Veronica. "You seem fairly close to him."

She supposed she was. "He's a good person. A little misdirected, but good."

That wasn't his point in making the observation. "Then why didn't you tell him who I was?" It seemed only natural that she would confide in Neil, especially after the man had made his not-so-veiled threat.

She bit her lip as she looked at Chad. Something had held her back at the last minute. She shrugged.

"Maybe your caution is rubbing off on me. For the time being, this is easier." She followed the thought a step further. "If Neil found out you were a private investigator, he'd want to help, and he'd only get in your way. He has a habit of being a little over the top at times."

That was putting it mildly. "How long has he been with that girl?"

She would hardly have called Josephine a girl, but under all that makeup and the volume of hair, she supposed Josephine was only around twenty-two or so. "A couple of months, I think. She's the flavor of the month." Veronica saw Chad raise an eyebrow in silent query. "Neil also has a habit of getting restless. He doesn't stick with anyone or anything for long."

That would describe a lot of men in his acquaintance, Chad thought. "Know her last name?"

Veronica shook her head. "I've only seen her a few times. Neil's never mentioned it. Since he doesn't seem to stay with anyone for more than a few weeks, I didn't think her last name was particularly important to know." Veronica glanced toward the closed door. "She looks as if it's a challenge for her just to remember to put one foot in front of the other when she's walking."

True, Chad mused. "I don't like leaving any rock unturned," he told Veronica just before the phone rang again.

This time it was hers.

Chapter 5

Hands shaking, Veronica placed the phone to her ear.

"Hello?" Straining every fiber of her being to listen, she felt her heart sink at the first words. "No." Veronica bit off an oath as she closed the cell phone. The two ends came together with a sharp snap like two sides of a clam.

"Wrong number," she replied to the silent question in Chad's eyes. Her own began to fill with frustrated tears as she stared down at the phone in her hands. She couldn't take much more of this. She'd thought she was made of stronger stuff, but she was wrong. She felt as if she was going to fall apart at any second. "Why doesn't he call?"

Chad knew what this was doing to her and how

frustrating and annoying it was to hear excuses. But
he wanted her to go on talking. As long as she
talked, she couldn't dwell on things beyond her
control.

"Could be he's having trouble finding a phone."
That was the most logical reason. "Or maybe he's
enjoying this." She looked at him sharply. Despite
her worldliness, he had a feeling she'd been shel-
tered from the world's dark underbelly. "Playing
cat-and-mouse with you might be a bonus."

"A bonus?" Veronica looked at him, confused.

Her mind didn't run in those channels, he
thought. His did.

"Might be someone you know slightly whom
you've inadvertently ticked off." He couldn't see
her antagonizing anyone on purpose. Or being
spiteful. There was just something about her that
told him that sort of behavior was foreign to her.
"More than likely, though, it's just someone who
hates anyone who's better off than they are—especially someone like you."

"Someone like me," she echoed.

Chad couldn't tell by her tone if she was bewildered or on the verge of being defensive. Maybe a
little bit of both, he judged. "Good family background, money, happy marriage."

To Veronica, it almost sounded as if he was de-
scribing someone she'd been in another lifetime.
She felt completely detached from all those
things—and horribly alone.

"My husband's gone. The happy marriage is

over,'' she reminded Chad. ''And it wasn't that easy to come by to begin with.'' Veronica closed her eyes, running her hands over her arms. And the pain it exacted from her when she lost Robert had been almost too much to bear. She was never going to allow herself to fall into that trap again. Better to remain distant and unhurt...

Suddenly she felt cold, so cold. Any minute now, she was afraid she was going to begin shaking uncontrollably.

Maybe because he was almost a nonentity to her, someone being paid to help her, someone she knew would be out of her life very soon, she heard herself saying things to Chad Andreini that she hadn't allowed herself to share even with her best friend. This was something she'd only told Stephanie and then later Robert, but not until after they'd been married several years.

Even then, she had been slow to bare her soul and her feelings to him. She'd learned to be cautious. To withhold her trust.

But right now, with her emotions being torn apart, feeling as if she was in the grip of something she couldn't begin to control, Veronica opened the door to her innermost world just a crack.

And let Chad in.

''Do you really think you know what it means to be someone like me, Chad?''

For just a second he found himself drawn to the look in her eyes. Surrounded by it. It took him a moment to pull back.

"Not firsthand," he allowed, surprised that he had difficulty shaking off the effect of her eyes. "But I know it can't be easy. Being rich has its own penalties. Anyone who thinks differently is a fool."

He surprised her. Most people just envied her, thinking she had the perfect life. Like the assessment he'd just made a minute ago.

"Being someone like me means never being sure if people are your friends because they like you or because they want something from you. Most of the time it's the latter." She sighed, hating this reality that was so much a part of her life. Being married to Robert had made her forget for a while. But it was something she had grown up with. Something that would have tainted and infected her life if she'd allowed it to. "It means having photographers pop up at the worst times, trying to get the worst picture possible to peddle to some tabloid so people can gloat and point, saying, 'All that money and see how awful she looks.'" Humor dipped in sadness played along her lips. "It means being lonely because you don't know who to trust, who to turn to.

"It means having people constantly after you for one thing or another and becoming angry if you don't come through the way they ask you to." But there were bright spots, and it was the bright spots she chose to remember. She couldn't have lived any other way. "Being someone like me makes finding someone like Robert almost a million-to-one shot— and that's being optimistic."

He had a feeling that she was. Despite everything. And that being an optimist was what was going to see her through this. "But you found him."

The smile now was still sad, but happy at the same time. "Yes, I did. And for however long it lasted, it was very good." And then Veronica sighed. "But it's over. And now all I have are memories—and Casey."

She felt the tears beginning again. For a second she fisted her hands at her side. So much for promises she'd made to herself, she thought. Sniffling, she brushed away the first tear, doing her best to dam up the rest.

"I'm not really like this, you realize." She fell back on a flimsy excuse they both knew wasn't true. "Maybe I'm allergic to the cologne you're wearing."

"Maybe," he agreed. It was time to get to work. He took a receiver from his pocket that was so small it could have passed for a wad of lint. "I want you to switch off your call-forwarding from your cell phone."

She opened her phone and punched in the proper code as she watched him attach something to the earpiece of the telephone on the coffee table. "What are you doing?"

"Putting a tap on your telephone."

More than likely, the kidnapper was taking precautions when it came to making the calls to her, but it didn't hurt to cover all the bases. Overestimating an opponent was as big a mistake as underestimating him. Chad wanted to be guilty of neither.

Finished, he took out what Megan, with her love of electronic gadgetry, fondly referred to as a decoder. He could feel Veronica watching his every move.

"When the kidnapper does call, we can pinpoint where the call is coming from. Just keep him on the line as long as you can." Taking the device between his thumb and forefinger, he held it up. It looked like a tiny monitor. "This doesn't take long to home in."

As if taking its cue the moment he said it, the telephone rang. Her sharp intake of breath accompanied it half a beat later. Chad held his hand up as he checked the panel on the device. This was the first time he'd used it. Megan had sworn to him this was state-of-the-art and foolproof. Right now he wished she was here to make sure it was.

The phone rang again. Veronica's hand hovered over the receiver. Her eyes were urgent as she looked at him. "He might hang up."

"Now." He pointed to the telephone.

Veronica jerked up the receiver. The moment she did, the line of ten digits on the tiny screen began whirling madly, chasing around as they searched for their proper positions. Listening to Veronica's side of the conversation, Chad kept his eye on the monitor.

One by one, the whirling numbers slowed down

and finally came to a halt. Forming a phone number. Creating a link to the kidnapped child.

"So," the voice on the other end grated metallically, "how are you holding up, Ronnie?"

Rage shot up through her, beginning at her toes and zooming right up through the roots of her hair, threatening to detonate within her. She struggled with the very urgent desire to shout curses at the kidnapper. But she knew she couldn't allow herself that luxury. Venting would only marginally purge her anguish and might come at a price too dear to pay. She had no idea who she was dealing with or what he was capable of. Casey's safety came before everything.

Her hands tightened around the receiver so hard she thought the shell would crack. "Not well. Is that what you want to hear?"

The voice began to sound more satisfied. Chad was right. This was a game of cat-and-mouse. And she was the mouse. "What I want to hear is that you'll cooperate."

Veronica could feel perspiration begin to zigzag down her spine. She wanted this to be over. "I already told you I would."

"Talk is cheap, Ronnie," the voice mocked. "The ransom won't be."

"I don't care. Whatever it is, I'll pay it." This was a negotiation. Robert had taught her that you never let the other side feel as if it held all the cards. But the kidnapper did. And she was no good at bluffing. "How much?"

There was a pause. One, two, three beats. Veronica looked at Chad, her eyes widening. Had she lost the kidnapper again? And then she heard the voice ask, "How much is your golden-haired boy worth to you?"

There was a noise pounding in her head. She could hardly hear. "I'll give you whatever you want. Just please—"

The kidnapper cut her off. "That's always nice to hear. How does three quarters of a million dollars sound to you?"

"I'll pay it," she said instantly. Veronica knew without stopping to think that she didn't have that kind of money in a liquid account. There was property plus stocks and bonds and treasury bills, along with enough red tape to keep three accountants happy. But all that could be handled. "But I'm going to need some time to get it together."

"Time, eh? Maybe you should think about auctioning off one of those paintings you've got hanging in the hallway. The Renoir'll get you that, easy."

Even with the metallic interference, she recognized the voice of pure evil. Was her son still safe? Had he been harmed by this madman? "Where do you want me to bring the money?"

The kidnapper was clearly enjoying himself. "Now, now, Ronnie, you're getting ahead of yourself. First, get the money and then we'll talk." The laughter faded, replaced by something that made her blood run cold. "Just don't take your sweet time getting it. Understand?"

She could feel fear sinking its nails into her again. The kidnapper was going to hang up on her. "Why can't you tell me where to bring it now?" she demanded.

"Because it's my show. And don't you ever raise your voice to me again, Ronnie. Or you're going to need tweezers and a magnifying glass to put your son together again."

Panic spiked right through her. "Please don't hurt him. I'm sorry. Please, he's only a little boy."

"That's better." The laugh sliced into her like a scythe. And then the line went dead.

"Hello? Hello? Answer me, damn it!" Veronica's head began to spin. She fought to keep from being engulfed by the sensation. "Answer me!" she screamed into the receiver.

Very quietly Chad took the receiver from her icy hands and replaced it in the cradle.

"We got him," he said.

For a moment, too numb to think, it was difficult for Veronica to understand what he was saying to her. Like someone encased in an impenetrable fog, she raised her eyes to his. Chad was holding up the tiny monitor for her to see. There were numbers across it. For the first time, she realized that there were words written beneath the first row.

She blinked, trying to assimilate the information. It looked like an address. "Is that where Casey is?"

He sincerely doubted it. But there was always a

chance. "That's where the kidnapper is calling from." Chad jotted the address down on his wrinkled pad as he began walking out of the room. "I'm going to go check this out."

For a second she stared after him, then came to. "Wait, I'm coming with you," she told him, hurrying in his wake.

Chad stopped at the door. He hadn't counted on this. The others had run into cases where the client had insisted on coming along, but he'd never had to deal with that problem. Until now.

He didn't want to be responsible for anyone else except himself. "Veronica, I won't lie to you. This could get very dangerous."

"Get dangerous? It already *is* dangerous. And this is my son who's in the middle of it. My son's in danger. What kind of a mother would I be just hanging back and waiting for him in my living room?"

"A smart mother." Her purse in her hand and clutching the cell phone to her, she gave no indication that she was about to stay put. Chad recognized defeat. "You're not going to be smart, are you?"

Reaching around him, she opened the door. "I already was. I hired you." She hurried out, then looked over her shoulder. "Now let's go. We're wasting time."

He had no choice but to take her with him, especially since she was leading the way to the car. "Yes, ma'am."

She had guts, Chad thought grudgingly. As annoying as her insistence to come along was, he had to admire her courage and determination. In her place, his own mother had fallen apart and continued to do so, according to Megan, until eventually, none of the pieces fit together anymore.

It looked like Casey Reinholt was a lucky kid. Now all they had to do was get to him in time to let him know that.

Waiting for her to shut her door, Chad started the car. The number he'd just gotten was located in Newport Beach. They were fifteen minutes away under perfect conditions. With one hand on the wheel, Chad pressed two numbers on his cell keypad as he backed out of her driveway.

A male voice answered after five rings. Chad had almost given up. "Ben?"

There was noise in the background. Chad couldn't quite make out what it was as the voice on the other end uttered a preoccupied, "Yeah?"

"This is Chad." Pressing the accelerator, he just managed to make it through the light before it changed to red. Chad kept an eye on his rearview mirror, watching for familiar dancing red and blue lights. "Are you on something right now?"

The laugh in response was deep and throaty. "Not yet, but I'm working on it." And then the humor left his voice. "Why, what's up? What do you need?"

What he needed was a chopper that could get him to the location in a matter of seconds, but he settled

for closer proximity. As he recalled, Ben's new
bachelor apartment wasn't located far from where
the phone call had originated. "Are you anywhere
near MacArthur and Pacific Coast Highway right
now?"

There was the slightest pause. "I'm having dinner at a restaurant about a mile or so away. Why?"

Dinner meant that Ben wasn't alone. Ever since
his divorce, Ben had gone at the single life with a
vengeance. As a rule, Chad didn't like asking fa-
vors, but this wasn't for himself. It was for the
agency. And a small boy.

"I need you to check out a location, and you can
get there faster than we can."

Reciting the address he had taken from the phone
tap, Chad went on to give Ben the particulars of
the case in succinct sound bites. He could feel the
tension escalating in the car with every word he
uttered, but that couldn't be helped. Niceties were
the first things discarded in kidnapping cases. The
only thing that mattered was finding the missing
child.

Chad heard movement in the background, accompanied by muffled voices. And then Ben came
on again to say, "I'm on it."

Veronica waited until he'd closed his cell phone.
"Who's Ben?"

Chad slipped the phone back into his pocket,
guiding the wheel with one hand. He barely
squeaked through another light.

"Another member of the firm." To get her mind

off what they were doing, he gave her a thumbnail history. "When Cade began the firm, he was on his own. My sister joined him within a couple of months."

The only thing Veronica knew about the agency, other than its phenomenal background, was that Cade Townsend had started it after his own son had been kidnapped. "Your sister works for Child-Finders?"

Changing lanes quickly, he threaded the car onto MacArthur. Lights from developments on the hills that bordered the road on each side began to go on as twilight pressed in.

"Megan's an ex-FBI agent." He didn't add that she had become one partially because of what he and the family had gone through. "My brother, Rusty, joined right out of college. Just before I did." For him, like Megan, it had represented a career change, a chance to do less paperwork and more good.

She'd been under the impression, when she had walked into the office, that it was a small firm. "So it's a family thing?"

He'd never actually thought of it that way. "I suppose," he answered.

The two years his father had robbed him of had taken away more than just time. It had taken away the security that filial feelings ordinarily generated. Even after Chad had been reunited with Megan, Rusty and his mother, it was never the same again. Not for him. The laughter was gone out of his life.

Oh, he loved his mother, as well as his brother and sister, as much as he was capable of loving anyone. But the betrayal he'd suffered at his father's hands had made him wary. It had taken away his ability to be in a relationship where all the guards were down.

No matter how hard he tried, the barriers were always there. Even if, by some miracle, they were lowered however slightly, they would spring back up at the slightest provocation. He couldn't get himself to trust, to relate, ruining any chance he had at a relationship, ending it before it ever got started. He caught himself looking at Veronica.

He was doomed to a life of distrust and wariness. A legacy he could never forgive his father for.

Changing the subject, he made an observation. "I was right."

Veronica turned her head and looked at him. "Right about what?"

"That the kidnapper is someone you know." He saw her brow furrow. She wasn't following him. He realized that he was skipping around. "The Renoir," he reminded her. "How else would the kidnapper have known about the painting in your hallway?"

She was about to agree, then stopped as she remembered. "The house was photographed for *Architectural Digest* the year Robert became chairman of the board at International Security. Anyone thumbing through a copy of the magazine in their doctor's office could have seen it."

She was right. Chad blew out a breath as he changed lanes again, passing a slow-moving compact. So much for that angle.

It brought him back to the theory that there was a certain amount of jealousy at work here, aside from simple greed. The kidnapper was enjoying being in control, enjoying tormenting her. Whether for personal satisfaction or to keep her off balance was something Chad had yet to determine. He had a feeling it was probably a combination of both.

Still, he couldn't quite shake the feeling that it was somehow personal. He let the hunch simmer.

Veronica tried not to let disappointment get the better of her. "Does this mean we're back to square one?"

He gave her what he hoped was an encouraging smile, at the same time surprised that he felt the need to do so. God knows he wasn't very good at it.

"No, it just means there're more squares than we thought."

She made no response.

The intersection of Pacific Coast Highway, more commonly known as PCH to those who were forced to travel it regularly, and MacArthur was busy that time of evening. Eager to make the most of the hours remaining to them, people were hurrying away from work, intent on getting home or stopping somewhere along the way at one of the numerous restaurants for an early drink to unwind from the day's pressures. Spilling out in all directions, the post-six-o'clock traffic made quick travel an impossibility.

Though he gave no indication of it, Chad waged a war with impatience as he slowed to a crawl less than half a mile from their destination. At this rate, he could have walked faster. He hoped that Ben'd had better luck.

Finally approaching the address he'd gotten, Chad saw Ben's car parked by the curb. All the other metered spaces were taken. His only hope was the parking lot on the corner.

Ben waved as Chad passed him. The ex-policeman was standing by a public telephone. Chad sighed quietly to himself. He'd had a hunch.

"We're here," he told Veronica.

She looked around as Chad guided the car to the back of the store, whose show window was filled with Oriental rugs. "He called from an Oriental-rug store?"

If only it was that easy, Chad thought. He'd seen the frown on Ben's face as he'd driven past him. That meant there were no viable suspects in the area. "I don't think so."

"Then where?" Lowering her head for a better view, she looked across the street. The intersection crisscrossed with three-lane traffic going in four directions, but there appeared to be a residential development in the distance and what looked like an apartment complex.

Stopping the car in the first available space, Chad

quickly climbed out. Veronica was beside him before he rounded the hood.

"There." Chad indicated the public telephone as they approached it.

A public telephone. It all felt so impossibly hopeless. Like searching for a toothpick in a pile of straw. "Can we dust for prints?"

"We will, but it won't do us any good," he warned her. "There's no telling how many people have used that phone."

Veronica's heart sank.

Chapter 6

Veronica focused on the tall, broad-shouldered man who stepped forward to meet them. He had a boyish look about him that seemed in direct contradiction to his eyes, which looked as if they had seen a lot. He nodded a silent greeting to her before turning his attention to Chad.

"Did you see anyone?" Chad asked.

Veronica held her breath as she waited for the reply.

There was a trace of genuine disappointment in his voice as the man shook his head. "Nobody who looked as if they were in a big hurry to get away from the telephone."

After seven years in the force, both in uniform and as a plain clothesman, Ben Underwood could smell a suspect a hundred feet away before he ever joined ChildFinders. The guilty were at times very adept at acting, but there was always some small thing that gave them away. He had scanned the vicinity when he'd arrived minutes after taking Chad's call.

He looked from Chad's companion to Chad, a silent question in his eyes.

"This is my newest client," Chad told him.

Chad glanced at Veronica, realizing she might take offense at the impersonal way he'd referred to her. But keeping a distance was what kept him sharp. Involvement of any kind tended to dull the brain and take the focus off what was important.

"Veronica, this is Ben Underwood. He's with the agency," Chad added, though he doubted it was necessary. As he spoke, Chad slowly scanned the immediate vicinity, looking for anything that struck him as out of place. Some minor anomaly that would register in the back of his mind waiting for him to work through. "Ben, this is Veronica Lancaster. Her son was kidnapped from a birthday party this afternoon."

All their clients were readily identifiable by the anguish in their eyes. This woman at Chad's side was no exception. Ben took her hand warmly in his, giving her the most comforting smile at his disposal. Like Chad, he'd been on the police force before he'd joined the firm. Unlike Chad, his time at ChildFinders had changed him from a man who kept his emotional distance from the work he was engaged in to a man who was moved by every case that came in, and not just those that crossed his desk.

"I'm very sorry, Mrs. Lancaster, but you couldn't be in better hands. Chad's the best. He's got an inside track on these cases."

The annoyed look Chad gave Ben was far from veiled. Veronica wondered at the comment and why it annoyed Chad.

"It's Ms. Lancaster," Chad corrected. "And thanks for coming out so fast."

Ben shrugged. "Hey, if I'd seen someone, then you could thank me." Ben shook his head as he looked at the telephone. "He's got to be a cool one, Ms. Lancaster, calling you from a pay phone in the open like that."

"The cool ones are usually the easier ones to catch," Chad pointed out for Veronica's benefit. "They get cocky, and sooner or later, they slip up."

He looked in the show window of the store. The glass was heavily tinted to keep the rugs that were hung on display from fading, but he could make out two men inside the store. Since they were behind the counter, he figured they had to be sales-clerks. Could be they saw someone making the call. It was worth a shot.

He turned to Veronica. "You have a photograph of Casey with you?"

Opening her purse, she took out her wallet and showed him. "I've got five photographs."

"Good." He nodded toward the store. "Let's go

inside and find out if anyone in the shop has seen him recently. Or saw the kidnapper making the call.'' He glanced at Ben. ''A man holding up an electronic distortion device to the mouthpiece of a phone's got to attract some kind of attention.''

''Not necessarily,'' Ben contradicted. ''You forget, this is a beach community. Lot of strange characters hanging around.''

There was that, Chad thought. But maybe they would get lucky.

Veronica caught hold of his arm. ''You think that the kidnapper had Casey with him when he made the call?''

''No.'' He doubted anyone was that cocky or that stupid. ''But maybe he lives in the area and passed by here on the way to his apartment. If one of those guys in there was bored, they might have gone outside for some air and seen your son in the back of a car.'' He looked across the street at the apartment building. The number of units was sure to come in at around a hundred, if not more. That made an awful lot of doors to knock on. ''First thing tomorrow morning, we need to canvass the area and pass around copies of Casey's photograph.'' That meant he was going to need help. Rusty was free, but he needed more than just one man. Chad looked at Ben. ''You between cases?''

Ben has been waiting for the question. ''Just. Wound up one this morning.''

''I'd appreciate an extra set of hands.''

''Glad to help. I'll check if anyone else is free,

too,'' he promised. He looked at Veronica. "I wish we could have met under better circumstances, Ms. Lancaster."

"So do I," she replied with feeling.

As Ben walked away, Veronica entered Ziev & Sons just ahead of Chad. The air inside the small shop felt stagnant and warm, heated, no doubted, by the hot words that were flying back and forth between what Veronica assumed was father and son. The two hardly seemed aware that there was anyone else in the shop until she and Chad were almost at the counter.

The arguing halted abruptly as the two men turned in unison away from each other and toward them. The frowns creasing both faces faded into smiles that were less than sincere, despite their width.

"How may we help you?" the younger one asked.

Chad produced the photograph and laid it on the counter. "Have either one of you seen this boy today?"

The older of the two men splayed his hands on the counter and leaned down to get a better look. He squinted, then shook his head. "No, I haven't seen him. Have you, Habib?" he asked the other man.

Habib picked up the photograph and studied it for so long Veronica began to hope again. But then he placed the photograph back on the counter and shook his head. "No. I am sorry."

Chad knew it was probably pointless to ask, but he had to. "Did either one of you see someone using the telephone that's right outside your store?"

"No. Is the boy missing?" Habib asked.

"Yes, he is," Veronica answered. "He's my son. Are you sure you haven't seen him?"

"Lady, I am sorry. All kids look alike to me. I do not know if I have seen him or not." He looked again at the photo, studying it intently. "But for sure not today."

Her heart sank a little lower as she tucked the photograph back into her wallet. "Thank you for looking."

The two men watched in silence as she and Chad walked out.

Once outside, Veronica drew a long breath, trying not to give in to the despair that hovered around her like a storm cloud. She looked at Chad as the door to the shop closed behind them. "Now what?"

He took her arm, gently drawing her behind the store, where his vehicle was parked. "Now we get you home. You need some rest." He held the passenger door open for her.

When she lowered herself into the seat, it felt as if her knees were buckling. "I'm not going to be able to sleep," she protested.

Getting in on his side, Chad started the car, then waited for a break in traffic before edging out. "Maybe not, but you can give it a try." She began to protest some more, but he cut her off, pointing

out the obvious. "You're not going to do your son
any good by running yourself down."

The short tether she had on her nerves snapped
again. "If you don't mind, I'd rather not be
preached to right now."

He spared her a look that told her he wasn't
about to get into any sort of verbal confrontation
with her. "No preaching. Just common sense."

Veronica turned away from him and looked out
the side window. What was wrong with her? He
was only trying to be helpful. Why did she keep
biting off his head for saying things she knew were
true?

"You know, I'm not really as bitchy as I sound."

He smiled in her direction. "Duly noted." He
saw her reflection in the window. He doubted if
he'd ever seen a sadder woman. Or one quite as
beautiful. "If it helps, I've known women who
seem a great deal stronger than you completely disintegrate when faced with what you're going
through. I think you're holding up pretty well."

"A Lancaster isn't supposed to disintegrate."
She could almost hear her grandfather's gruff voice
saying the words in her ear.

"What is that—a family motto?"

"Something like that." There were memories
waiting to get in. She kept them locked out. "My
grandfather told me that the day my parents were
buried. I was crying."

"How old were you?"

"Twelve. Stephanie was ten." And they had

clung to each other, afraid of what was going to happen next. Afraid of facing life without the parents they loved so dearly.

"Did your grandfather take care of you?"

"We had a nanny until we were sent away to school. Brighton Academy took care of us, if you could call it that," she replied. It all seemed like something out of another lifetime now. "My grandfather shipped us off to boarding school two days after the funeral. He didn't want to be tied down. Having us around interfered with his social life."

Twilight was weaving thin, dark threads over the area. She shifted in her seat to look at him, seeking some kind of assurance that would see her through the lonely, bleak night ahead.

"What did your partner mean by saying you have an inside track on these cases?"

He didn't like having the conversation swing back to him. He was far more interested in finding out more about her. Links to events could sometimes be found in the oddest places. He'd learned long ago not to disregard anything too soon.

"He's not my partner. Technically, we all work our own cases." That wasn't what she was asking. He was stalling and he knew it, but he didn't like talking about himself. He'd been forced to endure being the media's obsession of the month after his accidental return and then his father's apprehension and subsequent trial. It had forever forged a loathing of the spotlight.

But maybe she deserved to know a little about

the man she was placing her faith in, he thought.
Besides, if she really wanted to know, a simple trip
to the archives of any major newspaper could edify
her about his past. He could put a more honest spin
on it.

"My parents were divorced when I was seven.
When I was eight my father took me away. He
made it look as if I'd been kidnapped."

She stared at him. "Kidnapped? What about your
mother? What did she think?"

"She thought what everyone else did—that
someone had kidnapped me." The story had been
told to him over and over again by people who
meant well, people who had wanted him to know
what an impact his loss had been. But all it had
done was make him feel guilty that he hadn't somehow realized what was going on. Guilty for believ-
ing the lies his father had told him to make him
accept what had happened.

"My father played the part of the bereft, grieving
parent, even joining my mother in an all-night
prayer vigil. He was right there with her, handing
out flyers, talking to the police, pretending to do
what he could to find me, when all along he knew
I was living with one of his friends in another state.
I guess he did it to get even with my mother for
leaving him."

"When did you find out you'd been kidnapped?"

"Not until two years later. We had a big argument and I ran away from home. I hitchhiked
back." At almost eleven, he'd been resourceful.

Living with an alcoholic father had made him older than his years. "I had this crazy idea that I could move in with my best friend."

Curiosity and sympathy pushed her further into his story. "Why not with your mother?"

"I thought she was dead. That's what my father told me. That was the excuse he gave me for why we were moving away. He said that she and my brother and sister had died in a car accident and I was coming to live with him." He spared her a look. "At eight, you don't think your father's lying to you."

"What did your friend say when he saw you?"

"He turned white as a sheet. I thought it was just because he was surprised to see me. He went running into the house for his mother."

More than twenty-two years later, it was still as vivid to him now as it had been then. The yelling, the tears, his own bewilderment that gave way to shock and then shame at what his mother had gone through because of him.

"I remember she was my mother's best friend. Mrs. Mahoney took one look at me and sank down on the stoop as if all her bones had suddenly turned to water. Then she started laughing and crying at the same time, hugging me and saying it was a miracle." He remembered being smothered against the ample bosom and feeling loved for the first time in two years. "I had no idea what she was talking about. I thought everyone had lost their mind."

He sobered as he stopped at the light. "And then

I thought I'd lost mine when she took me back to my old house and I saw my mother. I hardly recognized her. She looked ten years older, twenty pounds lighter and so drained, like someone had siphoned the spirit right out of her.''

His mother had screamed when she saw him and then fainted. Megan had come running out of the house in response, and she stopped dead when she saw him.

Is it you? she'd asked in a hushed voice. When he'd nodded, she'd thrown her arms around him and held on tightly. *I always knew you'd come home. I always knew it.* That was the memory he treasured more than any other. That Megan had never given up hope, even after his mother had.

He had fallen silent. ''What happened to your father?'' Veronica asked.

Chad's face hardened. He didn't consider the man his father any longer, just someone who had ruthlessly used him as a means to get revenge. ''He was sent to jail for kidnapping. As far as I'm concerned, he stopped being my father the day he took me away.'' He felt suddenly awkward. ''I don't usually talk this much.''

''I'm glad you did,'' she said. ''I needed to hear something with a happy ending.''

He wouldn't have called it happy, or even an ending, really. As far as he knew, his father was still in prison. Periodically he received a letter from him. He'd recognize the handwriting and scrawl ''return to sender'' across the top, returning each one unopened.

No, for him there was no ending. Instead, it was an ongoing odyssey he was doomed to continue. His mother had never fully recovered, even after he'd come back. Not knowing whether Chad was dead or alive and fearing the worst had made each day of those two years a living hell for her. She still remained only a shadow of her former self.

Nobody should have to go through that, he thought, glancing at Veronica again. ''Anyone you want me to call to stay with you tonight?''

There were a great many people she could call, people who would gladly come and hold her hand if she told them what was going on. She was in the business of fund-raising for a score of charities and knew almost as many people as most politicians did.

But she didn't want anyone hovering over her with words of pity and sympathy. That would only make her crumble. She couldn't afford that.

Veronica shook her head. ''I don't want to tell anyone.''

Reaching the circular driveway, Chad turned off the engine and looked at her. He wasn't one for sympathy himself, but he judged that she was different. Women needed to be supported, to be bolstered.

''I could get my sister to stay with you if you'd rather not let your friends know about Casey.'' He knew he only had to ask and Megan would come.

With her husband Garrett's blessings. They were rare people.

This time Veronica looked determined as she turned down the offer. "That won't be necessary. I'll be all right."

Getting out, Chad came around to her side of the car. She had already opened the passenger door, but he took her hand and helped her to her feet.

The night was warm. Her fingers were icy. Chad caught himself thinking again how frail she looked. That same strange, protective feeling he'd felt before came over him. Without thinking his actions through, he raised her chin with his finger until their eyes met.

He could read every single thought, every single fear. For the space of a heartbeat, he found himself wanting to kiss her, to somehow reassure her that she was going to have that happy ending she so badly wanted.

He felt an almost disturbing tenderness. He'd never felt this way about a woman before and it bothered him more than a little. He shouldn't be having these kinds of feelings about a client. And yet...

"You know," he told her softly, "you don't have to be brave all the time."

"Yes, I do." The contradiction was quiet, but firm.

His duties did not go beyond her door, beyond their arrangement, yet he hesitated, unable to distance himself from what he knew she was going through, hating to leave her like this. "You're sure you don't want me to call my sister to come stay with you?"

She appreciated the offer and the concern that had prompted it. It made her feel less alone. But she needed this time by herself. To cry, to vent and then to put the pieces together so that she could somehow function. Because Casey needed her to.

"I'm sure."

He thought she was being foolish, but he couldn't force her to have someone stay the night with her. Taking out his wallet, he removed one of his cards.

"Here." He pressed it into her hand. "This is my beeper number, my cell-phone number and my private line at home. If you change your mind or need anything…"

She folded her fingers over the card. "There's only one thing I need. My son."

He nodded. "I'll be here first thing in the morning, unless there's a lead—and then I'll call you. Otherwise, you're going to need to go to your bank to get the ransom money."

Veronica nodded numbly. "Thank you."

He left before he was tempted to stay.

The expression on her face haunted him as he drove down the hillside. Chad flipped open his phone and called his brother. "I've just left a client, Rusty. You still want to see me?"

"Yeah."

"All right, I'm on my way."

It wasn't like Rusty to be this mysterious. As he

drove to his brother's apartment, Chad tried to dwell on that and not on the anguish he'd seen in Veronica's eyes. There was no reason for him to be this affected by her.

But he was.

Rusty opened the door to the second-floor apartment the moment Chad rang the bell, as if he'd been standing there, waiting. The smile that Chad would have sworn was eternally stamped on his younger brother's face looked strained. Nervous. Something wasn't right.

"Okay, I'm here." Chad looked around the small apartment. Nothing seemed out of order. He turned toward his brother as the latter closed the door behind him. "Got any beer?"

Rusty took a deep breath before pointing toward the kitchenette. "In the fridge."

"Looks about as bare as mine," Chad commented, glancing at the interior of the refrigerator. He helped himself to one of the four cans on an almost barren shelf and then popped the top. Straddling one of the two chairs at the table, he looked at Rusty as he took a long pull from the can. "You on a case?" He knew the answer before it was given, but it was a way to start.

Rusty joined him at the table, sitting on the edge of his chair. "Yeah, but I've got a little free time. Is there anything *you* need?"

He allowed himself a smile. Rusty always made

him think of an oversize puppy, eager to help. To do whatever was needed.

"I took on a case this afternoon. We have reason to believe that the kid might be being held in the Newport Beach area." He didn't go into particulars. With Rusty he didn't have to. Megan would have pumped him for every last detail. "Can you circulate a photograph around tomorrow morning? I've already got Ben on it."

Rusty looked relieved to be able to do something for him. His smile strengthened, just a shade. "No problem." Rising, he got up to get a beer for himself.

"Thanks." Chad studied his brother's back thoughtfully. Younger by six years, Rusty was about five inches taller and fifty pounds heavier. And right now, as tense as hell. "So what's the big mystery? What did you want to see me about that you couldn't tell me on the phone?"

"I could have told you." Can in hand, Rusty sat down again. "But I didn't think you wanted to hear it that way."

Chad could feel the hairs rise on the back of his neck. "Hear what?"

"Dad's out." Rusty watched his brother's face for a reaction. There was a flash of anger in Chad's eyes.

Very methodically, Chad set down his can on the table. He didn't look up. "My, how time flies."

Torn between loyalty and responsibility, Rusty gave him the rest of it. "He wants to see you."

Chad looked up sharply. "No."

Rusty knew that was what Chad would say. He also knew that Chad had never completely walked out of his personal corner of hell, because there were things left unresolved. "Maybe you should see him."

"No." The answer was firmer, louder.

Rusty leaned closer. There were times when he felt as if an entire generation separated them. Chad had always seemed so much older than him. "Chad, I'm saying this for your good, not his. See him."

"No." A shade of the anger he was trying to contain surfaced in the word. "There's nothing to be said. Whatever needed saying was said at his trial when I testified against him."

"That was twenty years ago. Things change." Rusty hesitated again, not wanting Chad to do anything he would later regret. "He says he's sorry."

Chad rose to his feet. He didn't want to take his anger out on Rusty. His brother meant well. But Rusty didn't understand. "He's a liar, Rusty. He lied to Mom, to Megan. To me. He would have lied to you if you'd understood. It's what the man does. He lies. I don't think he'd know the truth if it came up and bit him."

Rusty got to his feet, too, digging in. "But you would."

It wasn't like Rusty to push. That was Megan's forte. Chad narrowed his eyes. "What are you getting at?"

"The truth of it is, Chad, I think you need to forgive him. For your own sake, not his."

Chad shoved his hands into his pockets, fisting them. He laughed shortly. "I thought you studied criminology, not psychology."

"Can't have one without the other."

Chad's lips thinned. He'd only give Rusty so much slack. "Well, don't practice on me, Rusty. I'm not a case." He crossed to the door.

Rusty planted himself in front of him. "No, you're my brother and I can't stand to see you being eaten up like this because of what he did twenty-two years ago."

Very deliberately Chad moved him out of the way. "I'm not being eaten up. And I'm not about to absolve that man's conscience." He yanked open the door. "If he wants anything absolved, that's between him and his god."

"Yeah," Rusty called after him. "It is."

Chad just kept walking.

Chapter 7

Chad got into his car and slammed the door a little too hard. Despite his best efforts to shut them out, Rusty's words had gotten to him.

His first instinct was to go home. He'd put in a long, full day, and though he could work around the clock when needed, he wasn't a robot. He needed at least a few hours of rest.

But he was too wound up right now. Sleep would be hours away. It was always difficult for him to sleep, anyway. It meant relaxing his guard, letting go. It wasn't something he'd been able to manage with ease ever since that fateful day he had agreed to secretly meet his father at the skating rink. He'd ended up paying with more than two years of his life.

Besides, he thought, turning on the ignition, there was nothing at home for him. He wouldn't even have had a television set if Megan hadn't insisted on buying him one. He couldn't remember the last time he'd turned it on. The world was an intruder he preferred leaving at his front door.

So instead of turning his car toward his studio apartment located on the southernmost outskirts of Bedford, Chad headed back to ChildFinders. If he couldn't sleep, at least he could do something useful, do a little background research on the case. He wasn't adept at the computer the way Megan and Savannah were, but he could find his way around the Internet and its resources, given enough time.

The hall light barely ventured into the fifth-floor main office as he let himself in. Everyone else had gone home for the night hours ago. Unlike him, he mused, they had lives to lead.

Finding the switch on the wall, he flipped it on. Light blanketed the eerie shadows. He made his way into his own office, taking out the photograph of Casey that Veronica had given him. Rusty and Ben were going to need copies to circulate. He was going to place all his eggs in one basket and check out only Newport Beach for the time being, ignoring the other three areas where the phone lines had temporarily gone down. Going with his gut, he figured that the kidnapper wouldn't have driven far out of his way to make the call. Which meant that Casey had been somewhere close by when they'd arrived at the public phone.

Hidden in plain sight, he thought in frustration. He wondered if Veronica was going to get any sleep tonight. Megan had told him that their mother had seemed never to sleep those first few weeks.

He turned on the copier. Lights came to life and crept out the sides, squeezing between the lid and the glass. The gears went through their ritualistic groaning exercises before they were ready to work. Chad wrote notes to himself as he waited.

And tried not to think of a pair of worried eyes looking up at him as if he held the power of life and death in the palm of his hand.

Casey looked like her, Chad thought, studying the photograph. The same narrow nose, the same green eyes. He wondered if her smile was as wide as Casey's was. He hadn't really seen her smile, just a ghost of something fluttering along her lips.

The width of her smile had no bearing on this case, he reminded himself, wondering why the thought had even occurred to him.

Chad placed the photograph facedown on the glass and closed the lid before he pressed the number of copies he judged they'd need tomorrow.

He knew it was going to be a long night.

It had been a long night for both of them, he decided, looking at Veronica the next morning. It was a little after eight in the morning. He'd spent most of the night at the office. He'd napped on the sofa around three, then finally headed home for a quick shower, shave and a change of clothes. Veronica stood in her doorway wearing the same clothes she'd had on the day before. Her hair was undone now, lying loose about her shoulders.

She looked younger that way, he thought. More vulnerable. She looked like someone who needed protecting.

Something nameless stirred deep within Chad, a little more insistently than the first time.

He frowned, ignoring the nascent feeling. Feelings were best left out of this case. They had no place where gut instincts were required.

Her eyes were swollen. She'd been crying again. Chad's frown deepened. "Get any sleep last night?"

She blinked, feeling suddenly gritty and self-conscious. She rubbed the back of her neck with her hand as she stepped back from the front doorway to admit him.

"A little."

Very little, she added silently. She'd lain down on her bed, fully dressed, ready to leap up and leave at a moment's notice. She'd waited for the phone to ring. She'd waited for a miracle. She'd waited in vain.

Veronica closed the door and led the way into the living room. "I kept thinking I heard the phone ringing every time I started to drop off."

He didn't have to ask if it had ever rung. She would have called him if it had. Or, barring that, she wouldn't have been here.

Before he realized what he was doing or could

bank down the impulse, he combed the hair out of her face with his fingers. She mutely looked up at him in startled surprise. Chad dropped his hand to his side.

"You really should get some sleep," he said mildly.

"Can't," she murmured. "I tried." She lifted her shoulders in a slight dismissive shrug. "I'll sleep when we get Casey back." A silent prayer followed the affirmation.

Chad merely nodded as he glanced at his watch. Eight-fifteen. "Bank won't be open for another forty-five minutes." His eyes swept over her. Even rumpled, the woman looked appealing. But he doubted it was the kind of impression she wanted to convey to the bank president. "Maybe you'd like to change," he suggested politely.

Like a woman only marginally coming out of a trance, Veronica looked down at her clothes. Her appearance had been the last thing on her mind. Her expression was rueful as she raked her fingers through her hair.

"Maybe," she agreed. She began to turn, then stopped and looked at him. Her lack of organization was beginning to get to her. You never know how you'll behave in a crisis until it hits, she thought. Now she knew. And she wasn't very happy with herself. "Are you hungry? Angela's in the kitchen and can make you breakfast while you wait. I won't be long."

He wondered if their definitions of "long" were

similar. He doubted it. "I'm fine." He never ate breakfast. It tended to slow him down in the morning. "But I might get a cup of coffee if it's made."

"There's plenty." She'd poured several cups into herself already in an attempt to banish the haze around her brain.

He wasn't quite sure what made him pause to watch her as she hurried upstairs. Certainly watching well-shaped legs as she mounted the stairs didn't have anything to do with the case. Rousing himself, Chad made his way into the kitchen.

He wasn't as much interested in getting a cup of coffee as he was in checking out the housekeeper. Veronica had vouched for her, but Veronica struck him as the type to vouch for everyone within her sphere of acquaintance. As distrustful as she attempted to portray herself, he had a hunch that she hadn't a clue as to how dark a place the world could be. Money, or more specifically, the lack of it, could make normally good people do some pretty bad things.

And if you were bad to begin with...

He let the thought trail off as he entered the kitchen.

Angela Evans stood at the counter with her back to him. She was a small-boned, trim woman, and when she turned around, he could see she was probably in her late fifties. Her main physical attribute was her smile. She flashed it at him, taking his presence in stride. "May I help you?"

He detected the slightest hint of an accent. Southern, he thought. New Orleans, maybe.

"Ms. Lancaster said I might be able to get a cup of coffee. She's getting dressed," he added in case the woman wondered what he was doing here by himself.

"Poor lamb," Angela murmured with a shake of her head. She crossed to the far end of the counter where the coffeemaker stood. The pot was still three-quarters full. She got down a cup and saucer. "How do you like it?"

"That's okay." Very gently he maneuvered so that she was forced to step back. "I can serve myself." He saw no reason for her to wait on him. She wasn't in his employ.

The coffee was rich and dark as it settled into his cup, the aroma strong. Unconsciously he nodded his approval. He met her gaze as he raised his cup and asked a question he already had the answer to. "Have you been with Ms. Lancaster long?"

It was then he saw the sadness in the woman's dark eyes. "Only since she married Mr. Robert and moved into this house." Long, thin fingers took his arm in an urgent supplication. "Are you going to be able to find him? The baby?"

He set the cup down. "Baby?" he echoed a little uncertainly.

"Casey. He is my baby." The smile reappeared, smaller. Rueful. "My children are all grown and on their own now. Taking care of Casey was like taking care of my own again. Please, you have to find him before something terrible happens.'' The earnest look in her eyes gave way to something darker. ''And when you do, you will leave me alone with the man who has done this awful thing.''

A smile played on his lips. He admired people who didn't lie down and let life steamroll right over them. ''I think what you have in mind is against the law.''

''Man's law, maybe. But so is taking a defenseless baby from his mother. All I ask for is five minutes,'' she told him, holding up a hand to splay out her fingers. ''Just five minutes, and then you can have him.''

His nod was noncommittal, hiding his amusement. She made him think of a stick of dynamite, small but definitely lethal if lit.

''I'll think about it.'' He took a long sip of the coffee, letting it wind through his system. Feeling a kick. Man, he thought, two cups of this could get a car running. ''Have you seen anyone hanging around lately?'' He studied her as he spoke. ''Anyone taking unusual interest in the house or the boy while making deliveries, maybe?''

''No strangers. No deliveries. I do all the shopping for food myself.'' She gave him the impression that she had already gone over everything. ''The gardener comes by once a week, but he and his son have been taking care of the property for years now.''

''So you haven't noticed anything out of the ordinary?'' he asked again, hoping to jar her memory if there was some small incident she might have overlooked.

"I only wish I had." And then she looked past his head. The gentle smile returned. "You look very nice, Miss Veronica."

He turned around in time to see Veronica cross the room. She looked like a model for the cover of a fashion magazine. Except for her eyes. She couldn't mask the pain there.

Veronica squeezed the housekeeper's hand. "You don't lie all that well, Angela." Taking a deep breath, she turned to look at Chad. "All right, I'm ready."

It wouldn't take them long. He knew her bank's location. After all the time he'd put in at the office last night, he knew a great deal about Veronica Lancaster. Working the computer and its resources was far from second nature to him, but he was dogged about it, and eventually he had found the information he was looking for.

As the night had worn on, he'd pored over news clippings from the society page that dealt with her wedding and read the stories that documented both her husband Robert's untimely death and the funeral that had been attended by what seemed a cast of thousands from the social register and the world of high finance. In between, he read accounts of the parties Veronica had thrown while raising money for various high-profile charities. She was on the board of several national committees that concerned themselves with raising money for medical research seeking cures for half a score of diseases.

All his reading had brought him to the conclusion that Veronica Lancaster was ordinarily one busy lady.

A busy lady whose life had ground to an abrupt halt.

"It shouldn't take us long to get to the bank." He nodded toward the stove, endearing himself, he noted, to Angela as he did so. "Why don't you have something to eat?"

The suggestion had her pressing her hand to her stomach. She could almost feel the knot. "I don't think I could keep anything down."

He ignored her protest and looked at Angela. "Have any muffins in there?" He nodded toward the industrial-size, chrome-door refrigerator.

Angela gave a snort as she turned around and opened the refrigerator. "Mister, I have *everything* in there." It wasn't an empty boast. Every shelf was filled to capacity.

"And it can stay in there." Veronica waved for her to close the door again. "I appreciate your concern, Chad, but unless you want to spend time steam-cleaning your car's upholstery, I really think you should listen to me on this one."

Normally he believed in people making up their own minds about things. He had no idea what had him pushing the envelope with this woman. "A tank running on empty doesn't go very far."

"The fumes will see me through for a while,"

she promised. Veronica began to edge toward the kitchen doorway.

Angela stood in the center of the kitchen, her hands on her hips, shaking her head in disapproval. Her gaze swung to Chad.

"Get her to eat something," she implored him as he left.

"I'll try." Though he had serious doubts that anyone could get Veronica Lancaster to do anything against her will. He caught up to her in a few strides and opened the front door. "You told Angela." He wouldn't have thought she'd open up to a housekeeper, not after keeping her brother-in-law and her friend at least partially in the dark.

Veronica nodded as he got in on the driver's side. "I wasn't going to, but she's like a second mother to me." Or a first one, she added silently. She hardly remembered her parents. There was a vague feeling of well-being when she thought of either of them, but she had to concentrate hard just to remember their faces in her mind's eye. "And after meeting her, you can't still think she had anything to do with this," she added deliberately, watching his expression for some sort of indication of his feelings.

"No," he agreed. The housekeeper had impressed him with the depth of her feelings about Casey. "Unless she's one hell of an actress, she seemed genuinely upset about this." One suspect down, a hundred to go, he thought cynically. "I still intend to talk to your friend, Anne."

She nodded. "You're in charge."

He couldn't help wondering if she said that often to people. From what he'd read last night, he had his doubts that she gave up control easily. Which was why this had to be doubly frustrating for her.

Veronica looked down at the light gray briefcase she'd brought with her. Very gently she caressed it with her fingers. It had been a gift from Robert when she'd begun her fund-raising career. All it had ever held until now was a notebook and a few pens scattered about within its interior.

"Is this big enough?" It seemed like a silly thing to admit, given her background and her chosen career, but she'd never seen 750 thousand dollars in cash before.

He glanced at the case. "It's big enough," he assured her. "Unless you're planning on giving the money to him all in ones and fives."

She knew he was attempting to lighten the tension, but it continued to hang about her like a heavy shroud.

Afraid, half numb, half angry, Veronica stared straight ahead. "I can't believe this is really happening," she said quietly, her voice scarcely above a whisper. "I expected to get up this morning and find Casey bouncing up and down on my bed."

A vague image of Megan and him doing the same on a big double bed winked in and out of his brain. An almost faded memory. "Does he do that often?"

She smiled to herself, remembering last week.

They'd had cereal in front of the television set, dressed in their pajamas. "Saturday mornings. He likes me to watch cartoons with him." She pressed her lips together, the memory too much for her. She could feel the tears beginning to build again. She began to root through her purse for a handkerchief before she embarrassed herself. "Oh, God, I promised myself I wouldn't start crying again. I just can't seem to stop doing this." Unable to find a handkerchief or a tissue, Veronica wiped the corner of her eye with her fingers.

"I've got tissues in the glove compartment," he told her. Leaning toward her, one hand on the wheel, he reached over to the glove compartment and opened it, then took out a box.

She pulled a tissue from the box he offered her. Veronica sniffled, wiping away the remaining tears that were sliding down her cheeks. "You seem to think of everything."

He pushed the box back into the glove compartment, closing the door again. "Always be prepared," he replied, like a good Boy Scout. In reality, he'd never been a Boy Scout, never belonged to any organization that required socializing. That was part of the reason behind his quitting the force. He wasn't any good at the politics behind the job. He'd always done things his way, trusting only himself. That had rubbed his captain the wrong way. Chad had left the force rather than defend his actions. Defending yourself, explaining yourself, made you vulnerable, decreased your strength. So he was strong, silent. And alone.

"Are you?" she asked. He looked at her quizzically. "Always prepared?" she clarified.

He shrugged. "I try to be."

She blew out a breath, looking down at the tissue. She'd shredded a hole in its center. "Tell me, Chad, how do you prepare for something like this?"

The answer was frank. "You don't, not really. The best you can hope for is to roll with the punches when they come and manage to wind up on your feet."

He glanced in her direction. The breeze from the open window was playing with the ends of her hair. The way, he realized suddenly, he wanted to. His hands tightened ever so slightly on the wheel, as if that could somehow make him contain his thoughts and the feelings that insisted on infiltrating him.

"You left it down." Veronica looked at him, confusion in her eyes. "Your hair," he said. "You left it down."

Her hand went to her hair as if this was the first she'd heard of it. She looked almost surprised to find the soft waves touching her shoulders.

"I guess I did." The smile was rueful. "I couldn't think straight," she confessed.

"It looks nice like that." He wasn't accustomed to giving compliments. They didn't feel right on his tongue, yet she deserved this small thing he could do for her. "You should leave it down more often."

The surprise on her face blossomed into pleasure. "A fashion comment from a private investigator?"

For a second the pain in her eyes receded slightly. He felt a pleasant sense of accomplishment. "I'm trained to observe," he reminded her.

The compliment, tendered so simply, brought a comfort with it she couldn't quite put into words. She leaned back in the seat, watching the scenery pass. Trying not to think.

"It's too much trouble in the morning," she told him, seeking refuge in small talk. "I was considering getting it cut."

He kept his eyes on the road. "Don't."

The single word was almost a command. She looked at him.

He'd had a crush on a little girl when he was in the first grade. He'd fallen in love with her waist-length golden hair. He supposed that long hair somehow meant femininity to him. "A woman should always have long hair."

She felt herself smiling as she looked at him. "That sounds like something from the fifties." It didn't sound as if it should be coming from him.

He saw the bank up ahead and merged to the right. "Some things remain constant."

Very few things, she thought. Veronica slid her hand over her hair, looking at the building up ahead. "Something to think about," she murmured more to herself than to him.

Chapter 8

Jacob Browne's smile froze a little around the edges as Chad watched shock set in on the bank manager's face. The phrase "always a pleasure to serve you" was still lingering in the air when the granddaughter of Chester Lancaster and the branch office's largest account holder made her request.

Browne's eyes grew owlish. "How much?" he inquired in a disbelieving voice.

They were sitting in his office. The spacious room faced west, and the morning sun had yet to do more than hint at its presence here. The artificial fluorescent lights overhead seemed to cast a pall over the room as Browne continued to stare at Veronica.

Maybe she should have called ahead, Veronica

thought. But then there might have been questions she didn't want to deal with over the telephone. Veronica drew herself up in her chair, her hands folded over her purse. The cell phone lay silent, its telltale bulge just beneath her fingertips.

"Seven hundred and fifty thousand dollars," she repeated.

Browne's eyes darted from Veronica to Chad and then back again. Suddenly his face brightened. "This is a joke, right?"

"It's no joke, Mr. Browne. I need the money as soon as possible." She lowered her eyes to the briefcase she placed on his desk.

Browne rose to his feet. "But, my dear lady, that much money at one time... There are penalties, procedures—"

Chad cut the man short. "There is also a small boy whose life depends on it."

Chad didn't look in Veronica's direction. He knew she wasn't pleased that he'd said anything about Casey to the banker, but the gravity of the situation meant that they had to cut through any sort of banking filibuster Browne was about to launch.

The shock on Browne's face only intensified. "Is this true, Ms. Lancaster?"

"Yes." The sound of the word was almost too painful to bear. She longed in vain for the comfort, the luxury of denial. "If I don't have the money, my son will be harmed."

Browne looked at Chad suspiciously, as if to check whether or not there was any sign of duress between the two. Chad guessed that the man thought he was forcing Veronica to make the withdrawal. He wondered if Browne was going to give them a problem.

He pinned the much smaller man with an authoritative look. "How quickly can you get the money together? Cash," Chad emphasized. "Fifties and hundreds. Old, well-used bills. Not in sequence." The kidnapper would spot that immediately, and Chad wanted nothing to go wrong.

"It will take half a day. Two hours," he amended when Chad stared at him in piercing silence. When he continued to stare, Browne cleared his throat. "Maybe an hour and a half," he said, then qualified quickly, "But I'm not sure."

"See what you can do," Chad instructed tersely. Automatically taking Veronica's elbow, he helped her to her feet. "We'll be back in two hours."

Browne walked them to the door of his office, obviously relieved to see them go. "Yes, of course." Timidly he reached out and touched Veronica's arm. When she looked at him, he took a hesitant step back. "Ms. Lancaster, is there anything I can do for you? Anything at all?"

"You can make it an hour," she told him as she and Chad walked out.

"Yes, well…" Browne's voice trailed off. "I'll call you when the money's ready." he said before retreating back into his office.

"Well, he certainly came around quickly enough," Chad commented. He unlocked the passenger side of his car for Veronica, then opened the door before going around to his side.

"He wants to make sure I won't switch my accounts once this is all behind me." Veronica slid her seat-belt tab into the slot, subconsciously listening for the click. Her expression was philosophical. "People generally wind up doing what I ask them to." Her mouth curved ruefully. "Money's a powerful incentive."

He was a student of nuances. Of inflections and things left unsaid. He sometimes learned more about people by what they *didn't* say. "You don't sound very pleased about it."

"Well, I'm pleased that he's getting the money together to help me ransom my son, yes. But pleased that the Lancaster name has some little man in a suit that cost him over a month's salary jumping through hoops, no." A note of passion crept into her voice that Chad had a feeling she wasn't aware of. He listened all the more intently. "Just once I wish I knew that someone was doing something for me and not the money or the Lancaster name."

Closing her eyes, she sighed. A touch of bitterness entered her voice as she thought of the kidnapper who had turned her world upside down. She was complaining about trivial things. What if there hadn't been enough money to get Casey back? "I suppose there are far worse things to complain about."

He knew what she was saying. Funny thing was,

he understood. The truth becomes a desirable commodity when you're surrounded by nothing but lies.

"Yeah, but I can see your point." Feeling her gaze on him, he looked at her for a second. There was a warmth in her eyes. A yearning beneath the sorrow that almost took his breath away. He reminded himself of his position. "You want to feel people are being genuinely honest and up-front with you."

She would have said he was just paying her lip service, placating her like the others. But there was something in his voice that told her he understood. "Who taught you your manners?"

He blinked, broadsided by the question. "Excuse me?"

Even his question was evidence of his upbringing, she thought. He didn't just say, what? At any other time, she would have found that intriguing. Right now it was just a way to keep her mind off what she was afraid to think about.

"Your manners. You're awfully polite for a—" She stopped abruptly.

"For a what?" Amusement lifted the corners of his mouth. "A private investigator? We don't all chew gum, talk out of the side of our mouths and sound like Mike Hammer."

"Who?"

"Mike Hammer." The reference had just come to him. His father had had copies of the Mickey Spillane books lying around. Chad had read one out of curiosity, at the time desperately seeking some

common ground between them. "Private eye in a
mystery series written sometime in the fifties I
think. Never mind." Chad paused, turning down
the block. It was beginning to rain. He turned on
the windshield wipers. The rhythmic sound was all
that was heard for a moment. "My mother." He
saw that Veronica was confused. "My mother
taught me. She was very big on manners. 'Just because we're not well-off doesn't mean you have to
behave like you were raised by wolves.'" The
memory made him smile. "She used to say that a
lot."

She caught the note of affection in his voice.
"Sounds like she had a pretty good effect on you."

"She did." He looked at her. There were some
things he just knew, like the fact that Veronica was
a good mother. Too bad his instincts had kicked in
in his teens and not before. Otherwise, maybe he
would have realized what his father had been up to,
asking him to slip out of the house without telling
anyone to meet him at the skating rink. "Probably
like you have on Casey."

She was accustomed to flattery, to pandering
people who hoped to curry favor by saying what
they thought were the right things. He didn't fit that
mold. "How would you know that?"

"Call it a gut feeling."

He gave her no more of an explanation than that,
but there was something about the way he looked
at her. It cut through all her pain and comforted
her. More than that, it made her want to rest her

head on his shoulder and just let him take over. That hadn't happened to her in a very long time.

Veronica roused herself. The feeling was without basis. She was paying the man for his help, his expertise, and that was where it ended. She looked out the window, trying to guess where they were going. "So what do we do now?"

He updated her. "Rusty and Ben are canvassing the neighborhoods around where the phone call was made last night. I'm going to drop you off and visit your friend, Anne Sullivan."

Her body tensed instantly. She wasn't about to be dropped off. "I'm going with you."

Politely but tersely, he tried to dissuade her. "I think you'd be better off at home."

She refused to listen. "This isn't up for debate, Chad. I'm going with you and that's that." Her angry tone softened to an entreaty. "I can't sit home alone, waiting for the phone to ring, letting my imagination get the better of me—"

"There's Angela," he reminded her. "And the offer to get someone to stay with you still stands."

Sam's wife would be the perfect candidate for the job, Chad thought. He knew she'd be willing to help. It had happened before he'd joined the agency, but Savannah had gone through this herself. Except in her case, her daughter had been taken to fill a void in someone's life, not a bank balance. But the terror had been the same.

"No," Veronica retorted flatly, then added, "thank you. But I have to be with you. Besides,

Anne is one of those high-strung people. Especially now. If you come at her with questions, you might not get very much out of her except tears.''

He didn't like the sound of that. Chad spared Veronica another glance as the light turned green again. ''Tears?''

Veronica nodded. Casey's kidnapping had made her completely forget about Anne's heartache. ''Her husband, the plastic surgeon,'' she added in a cryptic tone, ''just left her for a younger woman. The improved, reconstructed kind, from what I gather.''

Chad wasn't sure he was following her. ''Reconstructed?''

''Plastic surgery from head to foot. She was his patient.'' She'd never cared for Anne's husband. There was something about the way he looked at people, as if he was cataloging their physical flaws and marking them for future improvement. ''Seems he fashioned the perfect woman, then fell in love with his own handiwork. Like Pygmalion.'' Veronica frowned, feeling sorry for Anne all over again. The woman deserved better. ''Anne's pretty distraught. It happened just two months ago. The party for her son was a way of trying to put it all out of her mind,'' she explained.

''I'll do my best to be gentle.''

There was no flippancy in the promise. She looked at Chad and knew that he meant what he said. ''I know you will.''

For the first time since she had taken the phone

An Important Message from the Editors

Dear Reader,

Because you've chosen to read one of our fine romance novels, we'd like to say "thank you!" And, as a __special__ way to thank you, we've selected __two more__ of the books you love so well, __plus__ an exciting mystery gift, to send you absolutely **FREE!**

Please enjoy them with our compliments...

Rebecca Pearson

Editor

P.S. A̶ value our cus̶ ve attached something extra inside...

FREE GIFT

Peel off seal and place inside...

How to validate your
Editor's FREE GIFT "Thank You"

1. Peel off gift seal from front cover. Place it in space provided at right. This automatically entitles you to receive 2 FREE BOOKS and a fabulous mystery gift.

2. Send back this card and you'll get 2 brand-new Silhouette Intimate Moments® novels. These books have a cover price of $4.50 each in the U.S. and $5.25 each in Canada, but they are yours to keep absolutely free.

3. There's no catch. You're under no obligation to buy anything. We charge nothing—ZERO—for your first shipment. And you don't have to make any minimum number of purchases—not even one!

4. The fact is, thousands of readers enjoy receiving their books by mail from the Silhouette Reader Service™. They enjoy the convenience of home delivery...they like getting the best new novels at discount prices BEFORE they're available in stores...and they love their *Heart to Heart* subscriber newsletter featuring author news, horoscopes, recipes, book reviews and much more!

5. We hope that after receiving your free books you'll want to remain a subscriber. But the choice is yours— to continue or cancel, any time at all! So why not take us up on our invitation, with no risk of any kind. You'll be glad you did!

6. Don't forget to detach your FREE BOOKMARK. And remember...just for validating your Editor's Free Gift Offer, we'll send you THREE gifts, *ABSOLUTELY FREE!*

GET A FREE MYSTERY GIFT...

YOURS FREE!

SURPRISE MYSTERY GIFT COULD BE YOURS _FREE_ AS A SPECIAL "THANK YOU" FROM THE EDITORS OF SILHOUETTE

Visit us online at
www.eHarlequin.com

call at Anne's house, she began to think that maybe everything was going to work out, after all.

Anne Sullivan was a small sparrow of a woman with voluminous auburn hair that swirled around her shoulders like a dust cloud at sunset. Her hands seemed to be in perpetual motion, toying with the ends of her hair, gesturing, straightening things around the den that didn't need straightening.

She reminded Chad of a woman on the verge of a nervous breakdown. There was no doubting Veronica's assessment that the plastic surgeon's wife was taking the pending divorce very hard.

A half smile flashed on her lips and then vanished. "I'm so glad you enjoyed Andy's birthday party enough to want to hire the same people. I have their card somewhere." Halfway to her desk, she stopped and turned to look at Veronica again. "But you weren't really here for it."

Veronica forced a smile to her lips, forced herself to sound as if her biggest concern was putting together a children's party. "Casey told me."

"Casey?" Anne echoed blankly as she stared at Veronica. The next moment she blinked. "Oh, well, yes, I guess a child could say that, couldn't he? Casey's a very intelligent, perceptive boy for his age. For any age, really. Not like my Andy." The laugh was nervous, indulgent. "Now, where is that card?" Gamely Anne rummaged through what could only, through the grace of charity, be called a mess. The smile she offered Veronica was apologetic. "I'm sorry, it's just that I haven't really been myself lately. Harold always insisted on handling everything. I'm afraid I'm not very good at this living-on-my-own business yet." Anne stopped. Her voice seemed about to break.

Doing her best to curb her impatience, knowing that what Anne was going through was painful, Veronica stepped forward and pulled the corner of an embossed letterhead out. There was a gay profusion of balloons running along the left margin. If held up, the watermark was seen to be a clown.

Just what Casey hated.

She looked at Anne. "Is this it?"

Still searching, Anne looked up absently. "What?" She pushed the glasses perched on the top of her head to her nose and looked more closely at Veronica's prize. "Oh, yes. That's it. Children's Parties, Inc.," she read needlessly. "They're really getting popular." She looked at Veronica in surprise when Chad took the sheet from her. Anne cocked her head as if that could make her absorb what was going on better. "Veronica, are you—" she seemed to search for a word, her brown eyes darting to Chad then back again to Veronica "—involved?"

At any other time, Veronica would have taken Anne into her confidence gladly and with relief. Their friendship went back more than ten years. But Anne had enough to deal with right now. No point in burdening her further.

So instead of telling her the truth, Veronica merely nodded. "Yes."

Anne took a longer measure of Chad before looking at her friend again. Her smile, still sad, was genuine. "Good for you."

Leaving, Chad tucked the folded letter into his jacket pocket. "I thought you said Anne was one of your best friends."

Opening her purse before she sat in the car, Veronica checked to make sure the cell phone was still operating. The screen declared it was receiving signals loud and clear. Why hadn't the kidnapper called back?

"She is."

Chad climbed in behind the wheel. "Then why did you lie to her about who I was?" After all, she'd told the housekeeper. Was there some reason she didn't trust one of her close friends as much as she trusted her housekeeper?

"It's easier this way," Veronica said, repeating the answer she had given him yesterday when he'd asked about why she hadn't told her brother-in-law who he was. "Besides, Anne's a romantic. She likes to believe that love can happen."

It was an excuse, but he let it go. Veronica was entitled to her own counsel. A distant curiosity prompted him to ask, "Are you a romantic?"

"No." She would have liked to have been, but that was her sister's domain. Veronica was the practical one. "But then Robert came along and showed me how good things could be with the right person.'' The mention of her husband's name brought a bittersweet feeling with it. Veronica let out a shaky breath. She looked at Chad. In a way, he reminded her a little of Robert. Except that Robert had smiled more. And laughed. God, but she missed his laugh. ''No offense, but I wish he were here right now.''

''Only natural,'' Chad allowed.

She had truly loved her husband—Chad could see it in her eyes. The thought nudged at the emptiness within his own soul, making him wonder what it was like to love someone that way, as if it consumed you. And to be loved. That kind of love for another human being was something he had never experienced. He found himself wishing, just for an instance, that he had. That he could.

They went to Children's Parties, Inc., and talked to the person in charge. Using the same excuse they had given Ann—and after some persuasion—Chad was able to obtain a list of the people who had worked the party at Anne's.

''This is highly irregular, you realize,'' the woman told Chad as she surrendered the computer printout of the names.

''I appreciate that,'' Chad replied formally. ''But as head of Ms. Lancaster's security, I need to run a check on all these people before they're allowed on the grounds.'' He pocketed the list. Stepping back so that Veronica could walk ahead of him, he nodded at the other woman. "Thank you. We'll be in touch."

He noticed the amused look on Veronica's face as they walked around to the rear of the store and the parking lot. "What?"

She shook her head, but when he raised his brows, she elaborated. "Nothing, it's just that you've gone from being my potential 'significant other' to head of my security team. I was just wondering if that could be considered a promotion or a demotion."

He sidestepped the question, not quite sure of the answer himself. It went to places better off untouched, he decided. "I have a hunch that anyone involved with you, Veronica, would want to be part of all facets of your life."

The fact that he hadn't answered was not lost on her. She wondered if he was just naturally evasive. "Is that a compliment, Chad?"

He hadn't meant it to come out as one. "No, just a simple observation."

Seeing a mall up ahead, he pulled into the parking lot and parked.

"What are we doing here?"

Pulling out his cell phone, he tapped in his office number. "I want to get this list to Savannah as soon as possible."

Veronica began to say something, but the phone on the other end was being picked up. Chad held his hand up, silencing her as he greeted Savannah and then read off the names to her. She'd taken them down, then told him that Erica Saunders—the woman Veronica said was being blackmailed—and her husband were away on a cruise. A sort of second honeymoon. The world, he thought, was a strange place.

Flipping the phone closed again, he looked at Veronica. "Now, what did you want to tell me?"

"Just that we could have faxed that to her." Veronica pointed to an office-supply store on the far end of the mall. "It would have saved you the trouble of having to read them."

He shrugged. "No trouble. I prefer avoiding things like fax machines if possible." Humor curved his mouth as he repeated something his sister had called him. "I'm technologically challenged."

Veronica was going to say that they would have faxed it for him at the store, but he'd diverted her attention with his confession.

"You can't be," she protested. "I saw you put that tracking device on the telephone."

"That was a piece of cake." A piece of cake he'd painstakingly learned how to slice by watching Megan do it for him several times. "And, as Megan likes to point out, even a chimp can be trained."

That sounded like something a sister would say to a brother. It made Veronica smile, remembering the way she and Stephanie had behaved toward each other before their parents' deaths. "Not very flattering."

"No," he admitted readily. "But Megan likes to stick to the truth."

Well, at least the man has no ego problem, Veronica thought.

Their next stop was the bank again. The money was waiting for them, stacked in random unmarked bills, just as Chad had instructed.

Thanking the branch manager, Veronica escaped before he could ask too many questions.

It felt as if all she was doing was getting in and out of the car, playing for time, doing busy work. And all the while, someone was holding her child, keeping him away from her. Maybe mistreating him.

A scream of frustration began to bubble up in her throat.

Though she was struggling valiantly to keep her mind occupied, Veronica felt as if her nerves, stretched to the limit, were about to snap.

For the third time since they'd left the house, she took out the cell phone and checked the screen.

Chad slanted a glance at the screen before looking back to the road. "It's still receiving."

She hadn't realized he'd noticed. Of course he noticed, she upbraided herself. He was *paid* to notice things.

Now she was arguing with herself. She didn't think she could take much more of this.

She threw the cell phone back into her purse. "So where is he? Why hasn't the kidnapper called again?"

Chad's voice was quiet, soothing, when he answered. "I told you, he wants to play mind games with you. The more on edge you are, the less likely the chances are he'll be caught." Chad made a right at the next corner. "We're going to your house to regroup."

"Regroup? I don't need to regroup." She wanted to take whatever was the next step, do whatever he thought needed doing. Anything to get her even an inch closer to Casey.

"Well, I do," he told her tersely, then added, "Humor me."

She had no choice. He was driving.

Chapter 9

The door swung open before Veronica could finish turning the key in the lock. Angela stood in the hall, her compassionate smile greeting both of them. The housekeeper asked nothing, but her eyes conveyed the foremost question on her mind.

Very slowly Chad moved his head from side to side. Angela's smile only grew more compassionate, more determined. She could offer a great deal of solace to Veronica, Chad thought. In his experience, women like Angela were rocks. He felt a surprising stirring of gratitude that she was there for Veronica.

"I have coffee, sandwiches," Angela informed them briskly, leading the way into the living room. She glanced over her shoulder to see if Veronica was following.

Feeling drained, Veronica walked into the room. She looked at the coffee table where Angela had placed the tray.

Coffee, sandwiches. As if this was some sort of social gathering she was organizing, instead of waiting to pay the ransom for her son. Tension overwhelmed her. Veronica stared at the neatly stacked, crustless quarters and broke down.

Reacting, Chad was by her side immediately. "Get me some brandy," he instructed a concerned Angela.

Then, because it was the only thing he could do, he put his arms around Veronica and held her. Held her until the sobs she'd allowed to escape dampened his shirt and faded. A strange, inviting warmth formed where her face pressed against his chest.

Angela hurried to the wet bar, taking out a decanter and a glass. "For you?" she wanted to know.

"No, it's for her."

Realizing that he was talking about her, Veronica tried to pull herself together. "I'm all right," she protested with more conviction than she felt.

"The hell you are." He held out his hand to Angela, waiting for the glass. When she gave it to him, he placed the rim to Veronica's lips. "Drink this."

She drew back her head, her eyes meeting his. The kindness there took her a moment to absorb. "It's just after noon—"

Why did she have to argue with him? "Veronica,

you need this." His eyes held hers, conveying things more eloquently than words. "Trust me."

Trust me.

The phrase echoed in her brain. Didn't he realize that she did? That she trusted him with the most precious being in her life? Her son. And she did not give her trust easily. But somehow this man with the stony expression and kind eyes had gotten to her.

Squaring her shoulders, Veronica took the glass from him. Holding it with both hands, she tilted her head back just enough to take a sip. The liquid swirled and burned a trail through her, waking up everything in its path. She felt less like crying.

"Better?"

She took a deep breath. Surprisingly, she felt less shaky, more capable of going on. The smile that graced her mouth was grateful. "Yes."

"Good." He took the glass from her and placed it on the coffee table. "Now sit down and have one or two of those undersize sandwiches." He saw resistance in her eyes. "Or I'll force-feed you."

Something told her that wasn't an idle threat. When she looked over her shoulder at Angela for help, she discovered that the housekeeper had retreated from the room. Resigned, Veronica sank onto the sofa. She still felt a little light-headed, but knew that the brandy hadn't much to do with the sensation.

She moved the napkins to the side but made no

effort to comply with his latest directive. "Do your duties extend to baby-sitting?"

"They extend to whatever it takes to keep the client conscious and functioning whenever possible." Since she wasn't helping herself to any of the sandwich quarters from the tray, he selected one for her. Taking one of her hands in his, he opened it and placed the sandwich quarter into it.

The amusement bloomed, reaching her eyes. He was awkward but gentle at the same time, and it touched her in ways she couldn't begin to put into words. "Are you going to make my jaw go up and down, too?"

He never hesitated. "If I have to."

She smiled in response. "You don't have to." Veronica took a bite. The bread stuck to the roof of her mouth. Because there was nothing else to drink, she took a sip of brandy to wash it down. He remained silently at her side. The word *faithful* whispered across her mind. "You're being very kind."

"Not a hardship."

The slight prick of self-conscious embarrassment had him looking away. Chad picked up a sandwich quarter himself, contemplating it before finally taking a bite. He was eating to keep her company while searching for a way to word something he didn't want to say.

Funny, wording things had never troubled him before. He'd always said what he had to say, directly and to the point, allowing the consequences to take care of themselves. Though he would never have been consciously cruel, diplomacy was something he never bothered himself about.

But she seemed so fragile he found himself worrying about the way she might perceive something if he was too blunt about it. Still, this needed to be said, needed to be cleared up.

"When the kidnapper calls, before you agree to make the drop—" he indicated the briefcase he had placed by the side of the sofa in case she wasn't following him "—I want you to ask him to take a picture of Casey holding up today's newspaper."

Veronica stopped eating. Very slowly, she set down the half-finished section and looked up at Chad with eyes that forbade him to continue. Forbade him to say why the photograph was necessary. She looked away from him. "All right." Her voice was reedy.

He wasn't exactly certain what came over him, why he suddenly found himself wanting to go the extra distance. A distance he'd never gone before, not with a client. He had no clue why this woman's tears were falling into his soul. But they were. He cupped her face in his hands, raising it until her eyes met his.

And, he made her a solemn oath. "It's going to be all right, Veronica. I swear to you, we'll get him back."

Silently, in the recesses of her mind, she blessed him for the pledge. She needed to believe him, to hang on to something until this ordeal was finally over. Otherwise, she wasn't sure she could make it.

Leaning forward, she brushed his lips with hers, her gratitude unspoken but not unfelt.

To say he was surprised was one of the biggest understatements of his life. So was his reaction to her kiss. A fire licked at his belly the likes of which he'd never felt before. Not wild and out of control, just deep. Bottomlessly deep.

Like the thirst he'd once had for belonging.

Caught unawares, Chad didn't drop his hands from her face. Instead, he held her there as the simple kiss deepened just a bit.

It might have gone deeper still, had the phone not rung.

The sound exploding in her brain, Veronica jerked back, her eyes darting around for where she'd dropped her purse. Chad was on his feet, retrieving it for her. Instead of combing through her things, he inverted the purse and deposited the contents onto the sofa. The ringing cell phone fell out, accompanied by myriad other things. Veronica snatched it up before he could offer it to her.

"Ask for the photograph."

The grim reminder hovering over her, she pressed the "on" button. She tilted the phone so that Chad could hear, as well.

"Hello?"

"Don't sound so breathless, Ronnie," the voice on the other end mocked. "Did you think I wasn't going to call?"

Strength. She had to come from a position of strength, Veronica told herself. Otherwise, the kidnapper was going to win. She did her best to sound calm. ''You took a long time to call back.''

''I was just giving you time to get the money together, Ronnie.'' The mocking note faded abruptly as the kidnapper got down to business. ''Do you have it?''

Veronica's eyes automatically lowered to the briefcase. ''Yes, I have it.''

''Good, then—''

Her heart hammering, Veronica looked up at Chad, seeking strength there. As if reading her mind, he nodded his encouragement. Holding the cell phone tightly, she took a deep breath, fortifying herself.

''Before I give it to you, I want to make sure that Casey's still—'' she couldn't bring herself to say the word that hovered on her lips. ''—still all right.''

''He's fine,'' the voice snapped impatiently.

She didn't want to anger the kidnapper, but Chad was right. She needed to know that Casey wasn't harmed. She needed proof to allay her own fears. ''No, I want to see for myself. I want you to take a picture of him holding up today's *L.A. Times*.''

''Look, bitch, this isn't some photo shoot you're setting up. You don't dictate to me, understand? This is my show.''

Veronica could feel every part of her trembling inside, but she knew she mustn't back down. This was important. She plumbed the depths of her soul for courage, unconsciously leaning into Chad, taking strength from the warmth of his body.

She raised her voice. "And my son, my money. I don't care where you leave that photograph, but I want it. Otherwise, no deal."

A string of obscenities came at her, making her wince. But she held her ground.

"All right, you'll get your damn photograph. It'll be on a shelf in the women's rest room at Westwood Park in two hours." The kidnapper paused, then added, "I didn't think you had it in you, Ronnie." The laugh would have been cold and harsh even without the metallic sound that vibrated in her ear.

The second the connection broke, she felt the room begin to spin. Perspiration came from nowhere, instantly drenching her.

Chad caught her just as her knees buckled.

Veronica could feel the contents of her stomach coming up her throat. A bitter taste materialized in her mouth. She tried to push him away.

"No, don't hold me," she cried. "I'm going to be sick."

Instead of releasing her the way she thought he would, Chad picked her up in his arms and carried her to the bathroom.

He set her down, and her feet had just touched the tile when the retching seized her. Rather than retreat, Chad flipped the toilet seat up and helped her to her knees. He held her hair out of the way as she purged the sickness gripping her insides. She retched so hard, tears came to her eyes.

Slowly the trembling began to subside.

Concerned, Chad waited a second longer, still holding her hair back, one arm around her waist for support. He'd felt every wave as it had come up.

Then, when it looked as if it over, he loosened his arm from her waist. "All done?" he asked.

"Uh-huh." Feeling as if she'd just been turned inside out, she didn't have enough strength in her body to give anything but a feeble grunt.

Carefully bringing Veronica to her feet, Chad pushed the lid back down and then sat her on top of the commode. He let the cold water in the sink run for several seconds before reaching for one of the embroidered washcloths on the towel rack. He glanced at the lettering as he passed the cloth under the faucet.

"Get a lot of people making off with your washcloths?" Wringing the cloth out, he placed it on the back of her neck.

The contact startled her and she jumped. She was only vaguely aware of his question. "What?"

"The washcloths—you have initials on them."

She tried to focus. "They were a gift from my mother-in-law. Subtle hint. She didn't like me keeping my name." Her fingers met his as she took possession of the cloth, bringing it around to her face.

When Veronica finally raised her eyes to his

again, they were clearer. She was beginning to feel human again. "Thank you."

Chad muttered something unintelligible in response. He'd never found a way to gracefully handle someone else's gratitude and mostly he ignored it. "Can you walk?"

"I think so." But she wasn't all that certain she could.

Before she could test her legs, he picked her up in his arms again. She looked at him in surprise.

Chad avoided her eyes. "Better not take any chances." He carried her back out to the sofa, thinking that he could have easily forgotten he was holding anything. If it hadn't been for the scent she wore. It seemed to be stealing into him like the mist at dusk. "You don't eat enough," he told her gruffly, trying to shake off the feeling that was stealing over him, as well. "You don't feel as if you weigh anything."

"Sounds like the voice of experience," she answered, still weak. "Do you carry women around often?"

He liked her smile. It did resemble her son's, he realized. "No, not often. You're the first. There's never been any need to." Placing her on the sofa, Chad glanced at his watch. "We have two hours. I'm going to check in with the office, see if anyone's made any progress. Why don't I have Angela make you some tea to settle your stomach?"

Veronica pressed her hand against her stomach. "I don't think I can keep it down."

"If you can't keep anything down, you're not coming with me."

She had no doubt that he meant it. "You can't get into the women's room without me."

"I'll manage."

"I'll drink."

Chad smiled, satisfied. "I kind of thought you might."

Savannah had already done a cursory pass through most of the names on the list from Children's Parties, Inc., when he called her. To his disappointment, but hardly surprise, there wasn't anything to go on, at least, Savannah qualified, not yet. There was still cross-referencing to do. But so far, there was no one with as much as a warning for littering. Nothing beyond a few traffic tickets blemished the records of the people hired by Children's Parties.

The only thing of interest, Savannah said just as he was about to hang up, was that Veronica's brother-in-law, Neil, was having difficulties with his creditors.

Veronica had mentioned lending Neil money. Maybe this deserved closer scrutiny. "What kind of difficulties?" Chad asked.

"The kind that has you looking over your shoulder every time you hear footsteps. Seems he can't pass up getting the royal treatment in Vegas. He's gone through the money he inherited."

''What about his trust fund? Veronica said something about his father having set one up for him.''

There was a pause on the other end of the line. When she spoke, there was just the slightest bit of amusement in Savannah's voice. ''Don't you usually refer to clients by their last name?''

''Lancaster, Veronica, same number of letters,'' he said. ''What's the difference?''

''Strictly speaking, Veronica's got one less.''

He knew she was ragging on him, that ever since she'd met him, she'd been trying to set him up with one of her friends. Savannah King Walters was one of those women who thought people should come in sets, like salt and pepper shakers. Chad blew out a breath. ''Tell me about the trust fund.''

Savannah got down to business. ''Still intact and ironclad. He's gotten as much as he can from that at the moment. The terms are pretty clear and pretty strict. Looks as if his daddy knew just what kind of kid he'd raised.''

''Yeah, maybe the desperate kind.''

Chad frowned, turning the idea over in his mind again. He couldn't shake the feeling that, despite plausible rebuttals to the contrary, Casey knew his kidnapper. And if he did, that made Neil their most likely suspect at the moment. He knew Veronica wasn't going to be willing to believe that the boy's uncle was capable of kidnapping him. But blood did not exclude wrongdoings. Neil apparently had motive; he certainly might have had opportunity and would have been able to take the boy without Casey raising a fuss.

"See if Ben can tail him for me."

"Starting now?"

"Starting now," Chad said firmly.

"You got it. I'll page Ben for you."

Hanging up, Chad paused for a moment, looking around the den. Two walls were completely lined with floor-to-ceiling shelves crammed with books. If they were Veronica's, she had eclectic tastes, he thought, reading some of the spines. They covered a broad spectrum of subjects. He barely had time to go through the newspaper in the morning.

Different worlds, he reminded himself as he walked out of the room. Completely different worlds. He and Veronica had nothing in common beyond their involvement in the case. If he felt attracted to her, it was just something he needed to deal with on his own. He couldn't allow it to go any further than it already had.

Veronica was still in the living room, curled up on the sofa and nursing a large cup of tea. Her eyes brightened when she saw him.

"See?" She raised the cup. "I'm almost finished." And then she saw the look on his face and her smile faded. She was on her feet instantly, fearing the worst. "What's wrong?"

"Just how well do you know your brother-in-law?"

"Neil?" Relief that this wasn't some dire news came swiftly. On its heels came a new wave of defensiveness. "No." She shook her head, adamant. "We've been this route before, Chad. Neil wouldn't harm Casey," she insisted.

"No one's talking about harming." Who knew? To someone as apparently irresponsible as her brother-in-law, the repercussions of a kidnapping probably never even dawned on the man. "Would he be capable of arranging something like this?"

She didn't even have to consider the answer. "All Neil likes to arrange are dates on his social calendar." She saw that Chad was unconvinced. "I'll admit he likes to go to Vegas and gamble. Maybe he even has a gambling problem." She hesitated, her loyalty torn, before confiding, "For some reason, winning makes Neil feel as if he's earning money on his own, instead of just living off his inheritance or trust fund. But he always manages to get back on his feet again. The periodic payments from the trust fund always come in the nick of time."

"Apparently not this time."

She didn't like the way he said that. "What do you mean?"

"He's in debt to the tune of a quarter of a million dollars."

"The kidnapper's asking for three quarters," she reminded him.

"Maybe he's saving up for a rainy day."

Veronica remained firm as she began to pace the room. "No, not Neil. It can't be Neil. He wouldn't do this." She swung around to face Chad, trying to make him agree with her. "I'd bet my life on it."

He tried not to be swayed by the look in her eyes. If it was Neil and he had betrayed the kind of trust he saw in Veronica's eyes, Chad figured he was going to grant Angela those five minutes alone with the kidnapper she'd asked for. "Would you bet Casey's?"

The color drained from her face. "I thought you just said he wouldn't hurt Casey."

"Maybe he wouldn't," Chad allowed, hating having to be brutal with her. But kidnapping was a brutal crime. "But what if he's not alone?"

Despite her resolve, she was beginning to entertain the idea. And hated it. "You're asking me to believe someone I've known for ten years, someone I've watched go from acne to aftershave, is a monster."

"No, what I'm asking you to do is consider the possibility and really give it some thought. Are you that sure of him?"

Her head was beginning to ache again, and she felt as if everything was closing in on her. It took effort just to breathe.

"Right now, I'm not that sure of anything." She raised her eyes to his face. "Not even you."

For a second they stood looking at each other, two strangers made into allies by a heinous crime, standing on opposite sides of a crumbling fence.

"That's the one thing you can be sure of," he told her mildly.

Yes, she thought, she could be. And she was pinning all her hopes on that.

Chapter 10

There was a pint-size baseball game going on in the distance when Veronica and Chad arrived at the park. Fathers and mothers could be heard coaching a collection of children hardly big enough to swing the lightweight bats placed in their eager hands. Cries of "Swing!" "Run!" and "Slide!" littered the air.

On the surface, Westwood Park looked not unlike the dozen or so other play areas that had been carefully carved out by the city council in the midst of developments within the growing city. There didn't seem to be anything out of the ordinary or sinister about the park.

But there was, Veronica thought. A kidnapper had traversed the grounds, placing a photograph in the women's rest room. Her son's photograph. Adrenaline pumping through her veins, she scanned the area, desperately trying to pick out the man who had turned her entire world inside out.

''There.''

Chad's voice made her jump. She automatically clutched his arm before realizing that he was pointing to a small brick building toward the left side of the park. The rest-room area. For a moment she had thought...

Dropping her hand self-consciously, she walked quickly to the structure just ahead of Chad. With each step she took, her heart hammered harder. What if there was no photograph?

She didn't want her mind to go there.

There was a rest room on either side of the southernmost wall, one for men, one for women. A public telephone sat between them. Unfinished garden apartments, in the final stages of construction, served as a backdrop. Similar dwellings, completed six months ago, stood overlooking the other side of the area.

Their kidnapper could be anywhere, though it was more likely, Chad thought, that the man was hiding somewhere in the construction site. Access was easy; so was flight. There were just too many places to hide, too many places to search.

He longed for a dog. A mutt like Jacques, part hound, part retriever. A wave of unexpected nostalgia hit him as he recalled spending hours with Megan trying to confound the dog with unique

games of hide-and-seek. Jacques was old when
they'd gotten him from the pound, but he'd had the
keenest sense of smell. He could find absolutely
anything they hid. All he needed was the slightest
scent, and he was off and running.

Jacques would have come in handy today.

Veronica turned to look at Chad, the breathless-
ness in her voice giving away her agitation. "What
if it's not there?"

"It will be," he assured her with the conviction
he knew she needed. They'd waited the allotted two
hours, timing their arrival to be just a shade after
the time the kidnapper had specified. She was hes-
itating, as if the extra moments were somehow insurance that the photograph was there. Chad looked
around. No one was approaching. "I'd go in with
you, but if there's anyone inside..."

She nodded. She hadn't needed anyone to hold
her hand since she was a little girl. "I'll be right
out."

He watched her disappear, his back to the construction site, careful to keep his body blocking vis-
ibility to the telephone. If anyone did see him, it
looked as if he was checking to see if there was
any change to be found.

The door to the women's room swung open
again. A young girl wearing a bright red Cardinals
cap gave him a mildly curious glance before she
dashed away, obviously heading for the game in
progress.

The next moment Veronica came out.

She was holding up a four-by-six photograph of marginal quality for him to see. Chad moved in closer for a look. It showed Casey, holding up a newspaper against his chest, and took up the entire frame; nothing else was even remotely visible. The kidnapper, it appeared, was leaving nothing to chance, no inadvertent clues that would give the location away.

Veronica saw what she needed to. "He doesn't look afraid." She studied the photograph intently. If she hadn't known that it had been taken by the kidnapper, she would have said that Casey looked very happy. "At least he's not being mistreated." Trying to remain hopeful, she surrendered the photograph to Chad.

When the telephone rang the next moment, Veronica let out a small cry.

"That will be our kidnapper," Chad guessed. "He's probably watching us right now."

Eyes wide, she scanned the area again as she brought the receiver to her ear. Where *was* he? Why couldn't she see him? Did that mean that Casey was somewhere close by, too? The very thought made her want to scream into the telephone, demanding her son be set free. But instead, she struggled to curb her emotions and remain calm.

"Hello?"

She heard something crackle before she heard the metallic voice. "Satisfied, Ronnie?"

She let out a shaky breath. "He looks like you're taking good care of him."

"Why wouldn't I?" the kidnapper mocked. "Your boy's worth his weight in gold to me."

Swallowing, she took a chance. "Can I talk to him?"

The request brought an immediate change in tone. "You're not in a position to make demands."

"It's not a demand!" she cried. For a brief second her eyes met Chad's. The sympathy she saw buoyed her. "Please?"

There was a pause and then a shuffling noise. Something she couldn't make out was being said in the background. It was muffled by more noise. And then she heard, "Hi, Mom." It was as clear as day, no distortion, no interference. Veronica's heart contracted.

"Casey! Are you all right, baby?"

There was no response. When it finally came, the voice that answered her didn't belong to Casey.

"That's all for now, Ronnie. Mustn't get greedy. You can talk all you want later. After I have my money. Bring the money to the Amtrak depot on Main Street at noon tomorrow. Put it in locker number 705."

"Tomorrow?" Her heart sank. "Wait—wait!" she cried, afraid the connection would be broken. "Don't I need a key to the locker?" She didn't want to leave anything to chance. This had to go off smoothly.

"So, you *can* use that head of yours." Hatred dripped from every mocking syllable. "You'll find the key taped to the underside of the telephone your hunky boyfriend's blocking.''

The connection went dead.

Fighting mounting panic, Veronica quickly felt around under the telephone's frame even before she hung up the receiver. Her fingers came in contact with something and she yanked it away. She held it up in triumph as Chad took the receiver from her and hung it up carefully.

''I got it,'' she said.

He made no comment. Instead, taking her arm, Chad quickly ushered her back to where his car was parked.

It was only when they were seated inside that he tossed something the size of a book of matches to her. ''Hold on to this,'' he instructed, turning on the ignition.

Still clutching the key in her other hand, Veronica picked up the device that had landed in her lap. She turned it over without recognition. ''What is this?''

''Another one of Megan's toys.'' He spared her a glance as they took a corner. ''We've saved the kidnapper's voice for posterity—and for Rusty to run through his expensive machines to see what he can come up with. My brother's hobby is playing around with audio equipment. Maybe he can find a way for us to figure out just who the man behind the tin voice is.'' He wasn't sure how that worked without a voice pattern to match it to, but if anyone knew how to do it, Rusty did. ''At least he might be able to clean it up enough to get a voice pattern out of it. Maybe figure something out from the background distortions.''

She hadn't even seen him put the device on the telephone—or remove it. To be that fast, he had to know what he was doing. ''I thought you said you weren't good with technology.''

He lifted a shoulder, then let it drop. ''I'm not. I just know how to push things into place.''

''No ego.'' She looked at him with quiet interest. ''That's rather remarkable, considering what you do and how successful you've been at it.'' Not to mention that the man was exceptionally good-looking, as well, she added silently, but that was something she wasn't about to give voice to. It was bad enough that she felt it, felt an attraction that couldn't have any place in her life, at least not now. She had no doubt he'd had his share of women make themselves infinitely available to him.

He saw no reason for what he'd just done to have fed his ego. ''Not my glory alone. We each work our own cases, but there's always back-up. No room for ego in a team,'' he told her mildly. There was no such thing as competition between them. Bringing home every missing child they set out to find was the only goal.

Veronica suddenly sat up, straining against her seat belt as she twisted around to look at him. ''He called you hunky.''

''Excuse me?'' It was obvious she'd gone off in

a different direction, but not one he could immediately follow.

"The kidnapper." Excitement built in her voice as she followed the thought through for Chad. "He called you hunky."

Stopped at a light, Chad tried to concentrate on what she was saying and not on the way Veronica's breasts were rising and falling.

"That means he could be a she, doesn't it?"

"Could be," Chad allowed, stepping on the accelerator again as the light changed to green.

"The kidnapper must have seen you. To call you hunky," she explained. "What do you think? Could he—or she—have been watching us at the park?"

"A very distinct possibility," he agreed. "The kidnapper's no fool. He—or she," he tagged on, giving her theory its due, "picked that place deliberately. There were any number of places to watch from. By the time we found which one, he'd have disappeared again, taking Casey with him."

So near and yet so far, she thought, trying not to let the desperate feeling take root again. They were moving this along. They knew the kidnapper's demands, knew that Casey was still all right and knew where and when to make the drop. By this time tomorrow, it would all be over, she promised herself.

She looked down at the small device Chad had passed to her. "Did this really record the conversation?"

"Should have, unless I did something wrong."

Though it wasn't likely. Megan had made it sound pretty simple. "We'll find out soon enough. I'll drop it off at the office after I take you home."

Veronica nodded, steeling herself for the ordeal of returning home. The thought of being there, knowing Casey was still somewhere out of reach, made it difficult to bear.

As Chad pulled the car into the circular driveway, he saw the other vehicle that was already parked there. "Expecting anyone?"

"That's Neil's car." She frowned and got out. She was no more up to seeing her brother-in-law today than she'd been yesterday. "God, I hope she's not with him."

"Josephine?"

Veronica nodded, taking out her key. "She's a little more of an airhead, a little more annoying than his other girlfriends. He's been with her for two months, which for him is a record. I think it's the novelty."

Taking the key from her, Chad opened the door. "Novelty?"

She found herself smiling at the gallant gesture. "She fronts a band. Plays guitar. Neil likes the idea of being on the fringe of show business."

"Ever hear her play?"

She shook her head. "No, just talk about playing."

When they entered the living room, Neil was sitting on the sofa, thumbing through one of the magazines on the coffee table. He was on his feet the instant he saw them. To Veronica's relief, Josephine didn't appear to be with him.

"Where's your lady?" Chad asked.

Neil looked affronted at the familiarity of the question. "Rehearsing." He addressed his answer to Veronica. "Been doing a lot of rehearsing lately. She has a gig coming up," he added proudly.

Veronica didn't want to talk and she certainly didn't want to talk about Josephine and the new-wave music Neil had raved about the other day. "Neil, what are you doing here?"

"Angela let me in." His tone was almost defensive. When he looked at Chad, there was distrust in his gaze. "I thought I should come by in case you'd heard something. Have you?"

There didn't seem any point in hiding this from him. After all, she'd told the bank manager, and the only vested interest that man had was the bank. "The kidnapper made his demand. Three-quarters of a million dollars."

Neil whistled in awe. "They don't mess around, do they?"

"No, Neil," she said wearily, "they don't."

Chad found himself disliking Veronica's brother-in-law, disliking the way the man almost mourned the amount that was leaving the confines of the family. He might care about his nephew, but he obviously cared about money more.

"So what are you going to do?" Neil was asking.

Veronica stared at him, wondering why he would even ask. "Give it to him, of course."

Neil looked appalled, and then he brightened, as if suddenly understanding. "Top layer the real stuff, newspapers underneath, right?"

"Wrong." Was he really saying what she thought he was saying? Did money mean that much to him? "Neil, this is Casey we're talking about."

"Yeah, right." He looked miffed at the implied rebuke. "But you've got to admit that's an awful lot of money to throw away without any guarantees, Veronica." He took a step closer to her, driving home his point. "Just because you give him the money doesn't mean you'll get Casey back."

Chad fisted his hands in his pockets. It wasn't up to him to tell the man what kind of scum he thought he was. He hadn't been hired to lay hands on undesirables who had nothing to do with the kidnapping. But his palms itched and he chafed against his own set of unspoken rules. This was personal, he reminded himself, and he didn't have the right to say anything.

He didn't have to, for Veronica did. "Get out," she ordered, her eyes blazing.

Uneasy, Neil stole a glance at the briefcase. "Hey, now, I'm only thinking—"

"—of yourself," Veronica finished for him. "You think that if I give that money away, you won't be able to ask me for it." She knew him too well to listen to any feeble denials. She'd closed her eyes to his weaknesses because he was Robert's brother. But this time he had gone too far. "Your only concern is the money. Get out, Neil. Now."

Panic had entered his eyes. He attempted to grab her arm to make her listen. "But—"

Chad moved in front of Veronica, blocking Neil's reach. His eyes were cold.

"You heard the lady. She's not going to ask you again. And neither am I." His voice was hard. When Neil made no move to leave, not out of defiance but out of sheer surprise, Chad grabbed the front of his shirt. "I'm guessing that maybe you're the type who needs to be shown..."

Fearful, Neil raised his hands before him in complete surrender. "Okay, I'm going, I'm going." He let out a sigh of relief as Chad released his shirt. In a last-ditch attempt to save face, he looked at Veronica. "But think about what I said, Veronica. Make the guy give you some kind of guarantee that Casey's alive, for God's sake."

Her brother-in-law had said more than enough to upset Veronica, Chad thought. Taking hold of the man's arm, he briskly escorted him to the door.

"You used to have better taste," Neil shouted to Veronica over his shoulder.

"If you know what's good for you," Chad informed him as he pushed him out the door, "you'll leave her alone." Striding back into the house, he met her stunned, slightly amused expression with a question. "Used to have better taste?"

"He's referring to Robert," she answered.

"Oh. I thought maybe he was talking about someone you went out with after Robert."

She shook her head. "There hasn't been anyone since Robert. I just haven't left myself open to anything." She was getting maudlin, she realized, and this was not the time to let her guard down. She didn't want him feeling sorry for her because she was inadvertently saying that she was turning to him. She was, but that was her problem to work out, not his. Veronica lightened her tone. "Besides, I've been too busy."

He accepted the excuse, seeing it for what it was. She was protecting herself. Not from him, but from pain. He understood that. Chad glanced toward the door. "It's none of my business, but I don't see how you put up with Neil."

"I do it because he's Robert's brother." She took off her shoes, leaving them where she stepped out of them. "He's not really a bad sort, just shallow. Besides, Casey likes him."

"He'll outgrow that," Chad commented, brushing off his hands without realizing it.

She noted the gesture and smiled. "It used to be worse." When Chad raised his eyebrows, a habit she found herself getting accustomed to, she elaborated. "After Robert died, Neil got it into his head that he should step into his brother's shoes." She shrugged dismissively. At the time, she'd found the idea almost comical. "Something like the prince trying to take over his brother the king's position. Neil was very serious about it. It took me a while to make him realize that it wasn't going to happen between us.''

She laughed softly to herself. Chad waited to be let in on the private joke.

''I think Neil had a difficult time understanding that, unlike the women he was accustomed to, I found him quite easy to resist. I mean, I like him, but certainly not in that way.''

He had no idea why that pleased him or why seeing her standing there, barefoot, struck him as vulnerable and stirring at the same time. But he knew he wasn't about to spend time puzzling it out. He had things to do.

''If you'll give me the tape, I'll take it over to Rusty before he gets busy with something else.'' He waited for her to remove it from her purse. Slipping it into his pocket, he crossed the room to the door. ''I'll give you a call if he comes up with something or if there's any news on our end,'' he promised, opening the front door.

She stood, debating with herself before she finally gave in. ''Come back.''

He stopped and turned around to look at her. ''Excuse me?''

Did what she'd said sound as pathetic to him as it did to her? But she couldn't help herself. ''After you drop that off at the office, come back.''

For a second he didn't see the point. ''There isn't anything more that can be done tonight, Veronica.''

And then he saw her eyes and understood.

''I know. I...I just don't want to be alone tonight.'' She ran her hand along the doorjamb, trying to still the nerves that had been jumping around these past two days. ''Maybe this sounds foolish to you, but I feel better when you're around. I feel that this nightmare will be over soon.''

No one had ever said that to him before. He tried not to make too much of it. She was under stress and he was a realist. Optimism came at a high premium, one that he usually wasn't up to paying.

But he found himself agreeing to her request. ''I suppose I can be your rabbit's foot for the night. I just need to stop by my place and get a few things after I drop off the tape.''

She nodded, placing her hand on the door to close it. He was halfway down the walk when she called after him. ''Chad.'' When he turned, she seemed to flush ruefully. The softest smile he'd ever seen graced her lips. ''Thank you.''

''Don't mention it.''

He was a man comprised of instincts, of hunches and gut feelings, and right now, all three were warning him that he was venturing into dangerous territory. Territory that was completely unfamiliar to him. If he had any sense, he'd back away and stick with what he knew. Finding kids, getting the job done. Not holding someone's hand through the night. He wasn't good at that, wasn't meant for that. Relationships, any kind of relationships, meant opening yourself up. Making yourself vulnerable. Waiting to be disappointed. He sighed.

He was making something out of nothing. The

woman was afraid and with good reason. If staying the night with her, if talking and figuratively holding her hand helped her through it, then he would stay the night. She was going through hell, and it was the least he could do for her.

He figured that was the end of it.

Chapter 11

He was being watched.

It wasn't anything Chad had detected out of the corner of his eye or in his rearview mirror. No suspicious vehicle tailing him, no glimpse of someone hiding in a doorway to set him off. But it was still there, that feeling. A strange prickling at the back of his neck, a tension in his spine that experience had taught him was his sixth sense.

Someone was watching him. The question was who and why.

He doubted it had been for very long. The feeling had kicked in just a few seconds ago. He was pretty sure whoever it was hadn't followed him from Veronica's. After all, he hadn't gone directly home. Stopping at the agency, he'd found that Savannah had gone home for the night. She'd left a note addressed to him saying she'd get in touch the moment there was anything to report. But Rusty was still there. The tape he'd left with his younger brother was as yet a work in progress, but Rusty had managed to uncover the faint sound of children laughing in the background.

"Might just be a TV on in the room," Rusty told him.

"Or the kids we saw playing in the park," Chad had speculated out loud.

Rusty nodded, getting back to the program he was painstakingly employing. "Or maybe something else," he threw in.

It was the "something else" that nagged at Chad as he drove to his apartment.

Just as the feeling of being watched nagged at him now. The stairs leading to his third-floor loft were out in the open with a view of the carport where he'd parked his vehicle. Chad took the steps slowly, thumbing through the flyers he'd gotten out of his mailbox as if they rabidly held his attention. Giving whoever was watching him the impression he was preoccupied.

When he reached the landing, Chad abruptly turned around.

And saw someone he'd just as soon forget standing at the base of the cement steps.

The figure was thinner, the shoulders slightly stooped now, instead of thrown back in arrogant pride. The face bore the mark of every one of the twenty years that separated then from now.

His father stood looking up at him.

Chad swallowed an oath. His first thought was that Rusty had given their father his address, but he knew Rusty wouldn't have, knowing how he felt. Neither would Megan. It didn't matter how Jerome Andreini had found out where Chad lived, he was here. And Chad didn't want him to be.

"What are you doing here?" The question with its dangerous edge was spoken barely above a whisper.

The older man flinched at the coldness that encircled each word. He licked his lips nervously, climbing a couple of steps. Still gripping the handrail, he stopped and looked up again.

"I came to see you. I thought maybe Russell didn't tell you I was looking for you."

"He told me." Chad made no move to unlock the door, wanting nothing to be misconstrued as a silent invitation. "And his name's Rusty. Everyone calls him that." His eyes narrowed in contempt. "But you wouldn't know that, would you? You didn't stay around long enough to learn anything about him."

Jerome licked his lips again, his breathing growing more shallow. "The divorce—"

"The kidnapping," Chad corrected coldly. "Whatever you didn't find out about your other kids was because of the kidnapping, not the divorce." The anger he was trying to keep in check simmered close to the surface. ''Can't exactly stick around and be a father to them after kidnapping the oldest, now can you?''

Bending even further under the contempt he sensed, the elder Andreini climbed the remainder of the steps, coming to stand before his son. Almost as tall, he gave the impression of being smaller. The years had not been kind. He began to reach out for Chad, then seemed to think better of it.

''The state's said I paid my debt.''

No, he wasn't going to be taken in, Chad swore. In his day, Jerome Andreini had been considered a charmer. Able to get what he wanted by his gift of gab and his attractive packaging. There was no evidence of that man now, but Chad had no doubt that, given the opportunity, the silver tongue would at least partially return.

He could go practice on someone else. There were no feelings worth saving between them.

''Well, the state's a little more forgiving than I am.'' His father opened his mouth to say something, but Chad didn't want to hear it. ''The state didn't lose two years of their life, didn't accidentally come back to the 'scene of the crime' without knowing it to see their mother so messed up she was on the verge of being institutionalized, now did they?''

The once bright blue eyes, so like his own, darted toward the door behind him. ''Chad, please, can't we go inside?''

Chad hesitated. Then, biting off a curse, knowing

he should just walk in and slam the door on this stranger with the same last name as his, Chad unlocked his door and left it open as he stormed inside.

He told himself he didn't want the neighbors listening to their private conversation.

Pushing the door shut again, Chad glared at the man who had both given him life and then destroyed a good part of it by what he'd done, not only to him but to the rest of his family. "Well?"

Jerome's breathing became more rapid, more labored. Perspiration popped out on his brow. Chad was moved by none of it.

"I never meant to hurt you, Chad. I..." Lost for words, for coherent thought, the man searched for both. "Divorce is an ugly thing. Your mother should never have left me. Never taken all of you away from me. I was trying to change, but she wouldn't stand by me." The excuses fell lamely from his lips, lips that had once been able to spin fanciful stories, trapping the listener. "It was your mother I was trying to get back at."

"Well, congratulations, you succeeded. And got two for one along with it. Quite a bargain." Chad shoved his hands into his pockets, suddenly seized with the desire to throttle the man who had caused everyone such grief. "Not hurt me?" he repeated incredulously, staring at his father in utter wonder. "Not hurt me? What the hell did you think telling me that my mother, my little brother and sister had been killed in a car accident was going to do to me? Make me snap my fingers and say, 'Oh well, we can always get another family any time we want one'? Your little fantasy ripped the heart out of me!'' he shouted.

Chad wrestled with the desire to throw his father out. Frustrated, he dragged his hand through his hair. He had some things to throw together if he was going to keep his promise to Veronica. ''What the hell are you doing here, anyway?''

Jerome's voice quavered slightly, then grew stronger as he made his request. ''I came to ask you to forgive me.''

Chad stared at him. The man had to be kidding. After what he'd done? Crossing to the door, he opened it again. ''Okay, you asked. The answer's no. Now get the hell out of my apartment.''

Jerome made no move to leave. ''Chad, I *need* to have you forgive me.'' In a desperate gesture he grabbed Chad's arm. ''Please.''

Disgusted, wanting to feel nothing but contempt, instead of the beginnings of pity, Chad yanked his arm away. His father stumbled backward, clutching his chest. A gurgling sound came out of his mouth as he stared at Chad, wide-eyed. Chad glared at him. He wasn't about to be taken in by any theatrics. He'd seen and heard too many of them in the two and a half years he'd been separated from the rest of his family. Promises made by his father as he swore off alcohol. Promises made to turn into something other than a weekend drunk who became mean at the first buzz. Promises as empty as the cans of beer that piled up on the living-room floor.

Chad waved a dismissive hand at his father. "Save the dramatics. They don't work on me anymore."

But when he looked, his father was still holding his chest, what little color there'd been in his pasty face draining. The next moment Jerome Andreini crumpled to the floor.

Now what?

Chad bent over his father, instinctively inhaling, checking for the smell of alcohol. There was none, but that didn't mean he wasn't intoxicated. Chad shook his father's shoulder impatiently.

"Get up, old man."

But the watery eyes didn't open. The breathing continued to be labored. With his forefinger and thumb, Chad opened one eye and saw the pupil was unfocused. His father had lost consciousness.

"Damn."

On his knees beside his father now, Chad felt for a pulse at the side of the man's neck. It was barely perceptible. Working quickly, he tried to remember the correct order of things from the CPR class he'd taken more years ago than he could recall. Hands on top of one another on his father's chest, Chad counted out the beats, pressing on each one. On five, he blew into his father's mouth. Nothing happened.

Annoyed at the edge of fear that began to scrape along his nerves, Chad repeated the procedure. Still nothing. "C'mon, old man, open your eyes. You're not doing this. You're not dying on my floor tonight."

Five minutes ticked by before his father came around and opened his eyes. His breathing still labored, he tried to apologize. "I'm sorry, I didn't mean—"

"Save your breath." It astonished Chad how easily he could pick his father up and place the man on the sofa. Taking his cell phone from his pocket, he dialed 911.

Finished, he tucked away the phone, then looked at his father, discomfort pushing its way forward. "I think you might have had a minor heart attack."

The older man seemed to be fading into the sofa's cushions, the very personification of exhaustion. A spidery hand that had once been so powerful covered his chest as if the gesture was entirely new to him.

"The old ticker don't work as well as it used to. That's why they let me out earlier." An ironic smile moved the corners of his mouth. "That, and good behavior." He tried to raise himself on his elbow to look at Chad, but failed. "I'm dying, Chad."

He'd just about had it with the tricks, the deceit. "What are you talking about?"

Jerome seemed to struggle to get his thoughts together. "Docs gave me six months. Maybe eight for good behavior." He smiled thinly. "That's why I've got to make amends." He reached for his son again, not making contact. "Make you forgive me."

It was a trick, another ploy by a man who was the master of deceit. Chad wasn't about to be taken in by it. There might be a sucker born every minute, but he'd done his time.

"Lie still. The ambulance'll be here in a few minutes," was all Chad could make himself say. Absolution wasn't within his power to give. Not with all the anger that was still in the way.

Because he called her, Megan came quickly, alerted by the tone of her older brother's voice before he'd even explained the reason for his call. She arrived at Harris Memorial Hospital ahead of Rusty. Her husband, Garrett, had wanted to come with her, but instinct told her this was something best kept simple for the time being. Chad was the one she was worried about, and she knew he would want the number of witnesses until this was sorted out kept to a minimum.

"They say it's his heart," Chad told her by way of a greeting.

"I know."

Their eyes met for a minute. She'd been his best friend when they were children, though he wouldn't have admitted it then. He'd taken her "death" particularly hard. "Why didn't you tell me?"

Megan touched his face, wishing she could somehow press peace into his soul. "I figured he would once he found you. I didn't want you having extra baggage getting in your way. You've still got enough.''

He saw Rusty walking toward them. ''Look, I'm on that case…''

Megan understood. She nodded, her smile encouraging. ''Take off. Rusty and I can hold down the fort, do whatever needs doing. No sense in you taking up space here.'' She touched his arm. ''Go take up space somewhere else. I'll call you if there's a reason.''

He should have left then, but he lingered a moment longer until Rusty joined them. ''Call me to let me know,'' he instructed.

Megan nodded.

''You look terrible.''

Veronica stepped back, opening the door wider. The man she had first seen at ChildFinders had been austere, formidable in his bearing and his presence. While still that, the man on her doorstep now looked drawn and just the slightest bit shaken.

''Bad evening,'' was all Chad said as he walked in.

He still wasn't entirely certain what he was doing here, even if she had asked him to come. Part of him felt it wasn't a good idea. Still, something inside him was glad he had promised to come by. He wasn't sure if he could handle being alone with his thoughts right now. Or even what his thoughts were.

By all rights, he knew he should hate his father,

hate what the man had done without regard to the repercussons. But the image of the man, old beyond his years, lying on his sofa clutching his chest, had taken the bite out of his hatred, leaving him with feelings he needed to sort out.

But not now, not tonight.

Closing the door behind him, Veronica tried to make sense out of his expression. She was almost afraid to ask, but she'd never been one who didn't face up to things, no matter what they were.

She caught his arm as he passed her. Chad looked at her questioningly. "Is it about Casey?" she asked.

Realizing belatedly how she would take his tense comment about his evening, he cursed himself for frightening her. "No. Nothing new. Rusty still has some cleaning up to do on the tape we got of your conversation with the kidnapper, but he thinks there might be kids in the background."

"Kids?" She tried to process the information, making sense of it. "You mean Casey might not be the only child that was kidnapped?"

With so much going on, that angle hadn't occurred to him. But now that she mentioned it, he doubted it. "No. Rusty played it for me. It sounds like kids laughing in the background."

She looked at him, remembering. "The park." Did that mean that Casey had been there, close by, all the time? She stopped before she could torture herself any further.

"Maybe, but I don't think so. We'll know more

in the morning.'' Maybe, he added silently. If Rusty had time to get back to the office. If something didn't happen to their father between now and then.

She showed him to the guest room. He set down the change of clothing he'd shoved into a gym bag before following the ambulance.

Veronica glanced down at the gym bag and wondered if he was just Bohemian or if he didn't own a suitcase.

''Are you hungry?'' It took him a minute to process her question. ''Angela made a pot roast. She said you looked like the meat-and-potatoes type.''

Meat and potatoes. No frills. What you saw was what you got. But not what there was, he thought. Because there were rivers of pain that could never be reached, never banked down. Seeing his father tonight had only reinforced that.

He shrugged carelessly at the assessment. ''I guess maybe I am.''

Veronica led the way down the stairs again, into the kitchen.

''No, I don't think you are,'' she said, taking the roast out of the oven where the housekeeper had left it warming. To her surprise, Chad took the roast from her. She indicated the dining room. Chad placed it on the table, set for two. ''I think that's far too uncomplicated an observation.'' She paused to smile at him as he held her chair out for her, impressed again by manners that society had all but mandated out of existence. ''I think you're a thousand-piece jigsaw puzzle.''

Chad picked up the carving knife left on the table and began to slice the roast. He offered the first slices to Veronica. "With some of the pieces missing?"

She pushed her plate toward him for easier access. "Not permanently, just long enough to defy labeling." There was a bottle of red wine standing between them. Angela apparently had second-guessed everything to perfection. "Wine?" Veronica glanced at the writing on the label. "They say this was a good year."

Having served himself some roast, he uncorked the bottle of wine and poured a glass for her. "Any year's a good one if you survive it," he said philosophically.

She watched him set the bottle down. "Aren't you going to have any?"

He shook his head. "No, I want a clear head in case our kidnapper decides he misses us and wants to chat." He didn't add that he almost never drank because his father had.

She knew she shouldn't have any, either. But the tension that gripped her body despite her attempts to relax threatened to snap it in two.

Because she seemed to want to talk, he let her dominate the conversation at dinner, commenting only when it was absolutely necessary. It was all small talk, and he understood that she needed to fill the air with it, to keep her thoughts at bay.

She surprised him by doing the dishes. After they

were washed and put away, she moved to the living room. He followed, bringing her unfinished glass of wine and placing it on the coffee table.

She sank onto the sofa, then wrapped her fingers around the glass as if it was some sort of a talisman. It was only her second glass of wine and she was accustomed to having far more than that without feeling its effects.

Tonight she wished she could drink enough to somehow deaden the pain, the fear that continued to war within her. But that wasn't her.

With a sigh, she let her head fall back against the sofa cushion and closed her eyes. "God, I wish this was over."

"It will be," he promised quietly. The kindness in his voice made her open her eyes again and look at him. "And then you and Casey will work at putting it all behind you."

She desperately wanted to believe him. But she was so afraid. So very afraid. Because she needed reassurance that someday her life would go back to being normal, she turned toward him. Her eyes asked for gentle honesty. "Did you ever put it behind you? Your kidnapping?" she added when he said nothing.

He knew that was what she was asking and knew what she wanted to hear. But it wasn't in him to lie. He hated the very idea. "I'm not exactly someone you'd want to use as a role model."

"Why not?" Her eyes held his as she tried to read his mind. Was that pain she saw? Or was that just mirroring her own? "You didn't put it behind you?"

He shrugged, wanting to look away. Being unable to. "My case is different from yours."

Every case was different, but this one had so many similarities, too. "You were still kidnapped. Still taken away from a home you felt loved in. Still had to deal with that."

Chad shook his head. "Different," he repeated adamantly. Seeing the surprise in her face, he softened his voice. "Casey won't be asked to forgive his kidnapper."

For a moment she didn't understand. Didn't understand that and didn't understand why the room felt as if it was growing warmer as she looked into his eyes. There was a fire in the fireplace, but if anything, it was burning down, not growing stronger.

"Your father asked you to forgive him?"

He found himself growing uncomfortable. Uncomfortable with the question and more uncomfortable with the reaction he felt whispering along the perimeter of his consciousness. A reaction to the woman sitting so close to him.

"You know, I don't generally get this personal with a client."

"You're not getting personal with a client," she protested softly, unable to look away from the bluest eyes she had ever seen. Eyes that made her think of the sky as it was on the verge of darkening. "The client is getting personal with you. Because she needs to.'' Veronica tried valiantly to keep the desperation out of her voice. ''Maybe talking to you is the only thing keeping me from going over the edge.''

He wished she wouldn't do that. Wouldn't place herself in his hands like that. It was one thing to do it with her faith that he would solve the case; it was another when she was offering him the broken piece of her soul.

''You're not the type,'' he told her gruffly, wishing she wouldn't look at him like that. Wishing he didn't suddenly want her the way he did.

Taking another sip, she laughed softly, shaking her head at the irony of his words. ''What do you know about my type? The society pages don't have a clue who I really am.''

There they were in agreement. ''Wouldn't think they would.'' He thought back to what he had read. ''Although there were some nice things said about your fund-raising abilities.'' She looked at him, surprised at the secondhand compliment. ''I'm basing my answer on what I see in your eyes. What I hear in your voice.''

Her mouth curved. ''When it's not quavering.''

''Even when it is.'' He found himself wanting to touch her face and wished now that he had taken her up on that drink. It would have been something to do with his hands. ''Strong is strong, and you, Veronica Lancaster, are a strong woman. You didn't cave in when the kidnapper called. Instead, you came to the agency.''

That didn't strike her as strong—that was only sensible. ''Because I needed a knight-errant to keep me from caving in.''

He'd never thought of himself as vain, but he had to admit he liked the comparison. ''Is that what I am? A knight-errant?''

She nodded, sipping again. The wine slid easily down her throat. ''Closest thing I've seen to Lancelot in my lifetime.''

''What about your husband?''

She paused for a second, casting Robert. ''He was more the King Arthur type. Good, intuitively smart, faithful.''

The Camelot myth had been Chad's mother's favorite. ''But the queen still strayed from him and went to Lancelot's room.''

''Yes, she did.'' Her eyes on his again, the words left her lips slowly.

The single phrase lingered in the air between them, as did the warm glow from the fireplace. Before sense prevailed, Chad leaned forward and took the glass from her hand. And then, ever so softly, he pressed his lips to hers.

Something flared within him, spiking high like a surge of electricity, leaping up before settling down again into the normal pattern.

Except that he wasn't settling.

He drew his head back before he was tempted to go forward. Without thinking, he ran the tip of his tongue along his mouth.

''I can taste the wine on your lips.'' He watched

her mouth curve in response. ''I said I wasn't going to drink tonight.''

Veronica's eyes never left his. ''I don't think what you find on my lips is going to impair your judgment any.''

He laughed softly. ''I'd rethink that if I were you.''

A spark flared in the fireplace, hissing as it fell back. Startled, she turned to look at it, her hair brushing his cheek. He felt his stomach tighten and realized that he didn't have a snowball's chance in hell of walking away from her at this moment.

The way he knew he should.

Instead, he weakened and gave in. Chad took her into his arms and brought his lips to hers a second time.

Chapter 12

It was meant, when he looked back at it later, to be a simple unguarded act of comfort. Though he had weakened, it was only supposed to be a soft kiss, nothing more. But the instant it began, it turned into something so much more. For both of them.

It was like touching a match to a long string of dynamite. The fire that ignited didn't extinguish. Instead, it traveled, moving faster and faster, to something that was far larger, far more encompassing than Chad had dreamed.

The stirrings he'd been vaguely aware of, trying to bank down and ignore, woke up.

Before the kiss flowered into something he wasn't completely incapable of handling, he caught hold of himself and drew his head back. His pulse slightly unsteady, he took hold of her shoulders. He looked into her eyes and found himself capitulating before he formed the first word.

This wasn't right.

"Maybe I'd better not stay."

Being alone last night had been almost more than she'd been able to bear. The thought of being alone again tonight drove shafts of panic through her. Her fingers tightened on his arms as she looked at him. "Don't go. Please."

"If I stay..." His voice trailed off, leaving the rest unsaid.

She knew what she was asking. Knew what would happen if he remained. But she needed his comfort, needed to have him here. He understood more than anyone what she was going through. If there was a price to pay for that later, so be it. She'd pay it. As long as she didn't have to be alone tonight.

"Please," she repeated quietly, her eyes eloquently supplicating.

He knew he should walk away. Here, now, he should just get up and leave.

But he couldn't.

The look in her eyes wouldn't let him. It held him prisoner.

His mouth went down on hers again, erasing the word that had lingered on her lips. He didn't want her to plead, didn't want her asking for something he was, heaven help him, so willing to give.

In less than a heartbeat, soft kisses gave way to passionate ones, and gentle touches grew into urgent caresses. It was as if there was a cauldron inside him, simmering for so long and now suddenly whatever had been within had expanded, boiling over. Drenching everything it came in contact with. Drenching him.

Chad tightened his arms around her as an urgency began to hammer away at him.

She hadn't been with a man since before her husband had died. Eighteen months. The responses that had suddenly woken up within her caught Veronica by surprise. Desires sprang up, demanding to be recognized. To be fed. As if she'd been on a prolonged fast and was now hungry beyond all understanding.

As his mouth fed hungrily on hers, as his hands, first gently, then possessively, passed over her body, a passion rose within her that made her head spin.

Veronica didn't recognize herself or what was happening to her. This was utterly new. She shivered as she felt his lips pass along her collarbone, his tongue lightly touch the tip of her ear as his breath set her on fire.

She had thought, until this moment, that she and Robert had had a satisfactory love life. She had thought that she knew all about lovemaking. But she was beginning to realize that she had only scratched the surface of what could be. She'd never felt her entire body ignite before, burning like a wild ember in the center of a raging fire.

All she could think of was that she wanted more. Needed more.

Her heart was slamming against her rib cage as he pulled her sweater up over her head, then tossed it aside. Having his eyes on hers made it that much more thrilling, that much more exciting.

The desire she saw in his eyes almost made her heart stop beating altogether.

Twin flaming arrows shot through her breasts as his palms rubbed just the tips of her nipples through the light fabric of her bra. They peaked, hard, tight, filling her with wanting. Wanting to feel his strong, capable hands take possession of her.

The next moment, the material between them disappeared with an adept movement of his thumb and forefinger. Her bra landed in her lap. Veronica's eyes fluttered shut as she absorbed the sensation of his skin against hers. She bit her lower lip to keep back the moan.

And then he was on his feet, carrying her in his arms. He crossed to the stairs. If there was a protest, it never had a chance to surface. His mouth was pressed against hers. Her head swirling, she had the vague sensation of being carried upstairs.

Entering her room, Chad set her down again, letting the length of her body brush his before her feet touched the rug. Then, slowly, methodically, as if this was a ritual that her station in life demanded, he removed her skirt and panties.

Her breath was coming in short snatches. With sure fingers, she grasped the edge of his shirt, pulled it away from his trousers and pushed buttons out of holes. She dragged the shirt from his shoulders a beat before he dragged her mouth to his, caressing her hair, pressing her body to his.

Together they tumbled onto the bed.

Passion exploded, rocking her as she felt first his hands, then his lips exploring her body like some undiscovered terrain. A kiss here, a caress there, heightening her excitement without cutting the edge off it until she felt like a mindless, pulsating mass of needs.

She twisted and turned beneath him, limp with pleasure and wild with anticipation.

He made her feel things she had never felt before. And mercifully he blotted out her mind as she was reduced to nothing more than passion and pleasure.

Quickly, outracing his thoughts before they could catch up to him and force him to stop, Chad dispensed with his trousers. He could feel his body heating to temperatures that couldn't be measured by instruments invented by man.

All he could think about was making love with her.

He knew he was breaking every rule he'd ever made for himself, but knowing didn't seem to help. He couldn't pull back, couldn't stop. Not even if his life depended on it.

It was as if he'd been waiting for this moment, this woman, this feeling all his life.

Desire had always been just a physical sensation for him. Now it was that and something more, something he couldn't define. Something he was afraid to define because identifying it would capture him even more solidly than this woman with the wide, vulnerable green eyes, this woman whose need ignited his own.

His lips were everywhere. Over and over again, he touched and caressed, fascinated by her reactions. Her soft moans heated his blood, bringing him up even higher. The obvious pleasure he heard escape her lips brought him a satisfaction of its own and made him want to heighten her reactions even more.

Though lovemaking was a pleasurable thing, Chad couldn't remember ever feeling this involved. Always before, there had been distance, a place to which he retreated while he watched himself make love to a woman. It was as if he could float above what was happening.

This time, there was no retreat, no safe place for him to stand off to. The ground had been taken away and he was free-falling along with this woman he couldn't seem to get enough of.

Chad passed the heel of his hand against her soft belly, pressing just enough to evoke sensations that made her twist harder against him. Made her grasp his forearms as if to pull her into him.

He brought his mouth down to where his hand had been and felt her flesh quiver beneath his lips.

She tasted of innocence, of things he'd never tasted before.

Ridiculous thought, given who she was and that she had a child.

But the word *innocence* continued to echo in his brain, making him humble for the gift he was sharing.

Making him proud.

He did what he could to bring her to the crest of fulfillment first. It wasn't hard to know the exact moment it happened. There were no games. She wasn't coy. He found himself enjoying the way her eyes flew open the first time the explosion flowered within her.

Chad felt her nails digging into his shoulders as she arched to absorb the core of the storm. His own desire grew exponentially until he was completely intoxicated with it. And besotted with her.

He couldn't hold back any longer.

With her breath rasping against his ear, warming his blood even more, Chad drove himself into her. He muffled her cries with his mouth as his hips melded with hers. The last dance had begun. A dance that was theirs alone.

Poised above her, trying to balance himself so that he wouldn't hurt her, Chad grabbed fistfuls of sheet beneath his hands as the final thrust brought the elusive, sought-after sensation.

Formless words came to him, floating through his brain, shimmering just out of reach.

And then euphoria blanketed him and, with it, a

sense of profound contentment. It took him a moment to identify the feeling. Another to examine it in awed wonder. He'd never experienced that before.

After lovemaking there had always been a sense of exhaustion, perhaps with it a desire to sleep. But never anything further. Nothing like...whatever this was.

He pushed it back, not wanting to examine it too closely. Afraid of losing it. Afraid of wanting to find it again.

He realized that he had his arm around her and was holding her close against his side.

"Was I all right?" she asked.

The question, quiet, shy, honest, cut through the haze that was still clinging to his brain. It took him a second to make sense of it.

When he did, Chad felt something akin to a chuckle in his chest and wondered at it. He wasn't a man given to things like chuckling. But the question struck him as amusing. Didn't she realize that she'd all but made the walls shake around them? That even now, with her against him, he felt the distant lick of appetites beginning all over again, he, who was always satisfied to make love only once?

"Only if the gods of the dictionary decide to write an entirely new definition of the expression *all right*." He cradled her to him so that he could look down into her face. She *was* serious, he thought. The chuckle faded. "Why? Did I give you any cause to doubt that you were anything but magnificent?''

She blushed then. Like a schoolgirl, he thought. There was nothing of the sophisticated socialite here in his arms. Only a woman who could have easily had a battalion of men eagerly jumping through hoops to sample just a little of what he'd just had.

Veronica hesitated, the blush deepening. ''It's just that I'm not very experienced. I mean, other than Robert, I didn't... And then Robert...he was a very good lover, but he wasn't...'' This wasn't coming out right, she thought. Chad probably thought she was an idiot. She finally found the word she was looking for—or at least one that was close. ''Energetic.'' She lowered her eyes, embarrassed to look at him. ''I just wanted to know if I satisfied you.''

''Satisfied me?'' He rolled the term around on his tongue, wondering again how she could possibly be serious. ''Yes and no.''

''Yes and no?''

Turning suddenly, Chad was over her again, his hands framing her head, his eyes looking into hers. His body intimately touching hers and heating quickly. Damn, but he wanted her again.

One for the books, he thought.

''Yes, you satisfied me. More than satisfied me,'' he said. ''But you also made me want more.'' Ever so lightly, he began to kiss her lips again, first the upper, then the lower. He heard her sigh of surrender, and his blood began to surge again, pulsing to his loins. "Hence," he breathed, barely passing his tongue along both her lips, "yes and no."

Her body awakened again, she moved beneath him, silently extending a welcoming to the invitation she had received. "Oh, now I understand."

"As long as we're clear."

"Very." Entwining her arms around his neck, Veronica raised her lips to his, capturing them. Capturing him. And slipping gladly back into paradise for a second time.

She'd always been a quick riser. Unlike her younger sister, Veronica popped up out of bed like bread from a toaster. But this time she was reluctant to leave the sheltering arms of sleep behind. She'd spent what little there'd been left of the night reliving their lovemaking in her dreams, and the netherworld was much more preferable to the world that waited to greet her at first light.

But her inner clock was preset and roused the rest of her. Slowly she opened her eyes and realized that morning had joined them, dressed in full regalia. Surprised that she had slept in, Veronica tried to focus on her surroundings.

Chad was already up on his side of the bed, slipping his jeans on over hips unencumbered by underwear. She felt her cheeks heating right along with the rest of her body.

The part of her that had always been reserved couldn't believe what had happened last night.

Couldn't believe that she had made love with a man she hardly knew.

But another part of her, the more recessed, sensitive part, felt as if she had known him forever. As if she had been waiting for him forever. Waiting for a man who could take care of her. Who made love with wild, passionate abandonment. To her, not her name, not her money, but to her.

Had she really found him? Had he somehow managed to wander in and find her amid all this chaos going on around her?

It was too soon, too early for answers. Only questions. Pulling the sheet to her, Veronica sat up. Her hair cascaded in uncombed waves around her shoulders. She glanced to where the clock usually was. The space was empty. Vaguely she remembered accidentally flinging out her hand and hitting it during a crucial moment. It had toppled over and was probably somewhere under the bed.

''What time is it?'' she asked.

His back to her, Chad raised his head. He'd been hoping to make it out of the room before she woke up. It would have been easier that way.

He turned to face her, not knowing what he would see in her eyes. Recrimination? Denial? Anger? She was entitled to all of those and more. Conduct Unbecoming—that was what they would have labeled it if he'd still been in law enforcement. He'd taken advantage of her last night, of her vulnerability and of whatever it was that felt lacking within himself.

But dawn brought reason in tow.

And reason brought guilt with it. The excuses he'd given himself had trouble holding up in the light of day.

Guilt or not, he wanted her again. The sun was dancing along her tousled hair, grazing her exposed skin. Sleep was still outlining her eyes, and if he looked, he could see the swell of her breasts against the thin sheet. The outline of her leg tempted him to reach out and touch her again, the way he had last night. To caress what had been his for a blink of an eye. What couldn't be his in the day-to-day world they occupied.

Just looking at her made his mouth go dry.

So Chad looked away, pretending to cast his gaze around for his shoes. "Almost seven o'clock. Your housekeeper will be here soon."

She knew what time Angela arrived. Was he getting up because he didn't want to be caught in bed with her? Or was it her reputation he was concerned about? The thought brought a sweetness in its wake. For all his tough exterior, the man was old-fashioned. But then, his manners had hinted at that.

"Angela has her own key," she told him softly.

"My point exactly." Rising, he stepped into his shoes. "You don't want her coming up here and finding you with me."

Her private life had always been that, as private as she could keep it. And though she cared about Angela and regarded her as something more than just a housekeeper, she wouldn't have openly flaunted this before the woman. Still, there was something in Chad's tone that caught her attention. She could feel her spine tensing.

"Why?"

He looked at her face, purposely keeping his eyes from the rest of her. "Because I'm the 'hired help.'"

It *was* her reputation he was worried about. She was touched.

Rising to her knees, Veronica reached up and cupped his cheek with her hand. "You're not the hired help, Chad. You're a kind, giving man who tried to help me make it through the night." Her words echoed back to her, and she realized how he would interpret them. That last night had been a one-night stand, born of desperation. "And it wasn't a panic attack last night, Chad. It wasn't a choice between you and a tranquilizer." The expression in his eyes told her she'd guessed his reaction correctly. Her mouth curved into a smile. "Although the final effect was probably pretty close. I never, ever do what I don't want to."

Tucking the sheet around her, she looked at him intently. Her gaze held his.

"Know this," she said. "I'm not holding you to a single thing, but for me, last night was very special."

He wanted to tell her that it had been the same for him. That what he had experienced last night had never come his way before. That he had felt something he had never thought he would.

But the words refused to come to his lips. Because if they did, he would be tempted to think that there could be something between them. And there couldn't. Not because of who she was but because of what *he* was. A man whose past had such a grip on his present that it refused to allow him to feel things normal men did. Refused to allow him to have the normal life other men had. If something more was allowed to grow between them, she would be the victim here. And he had been hired to keep her from being a victim of any kind.

Even *his* victim.

So, instead, he looked away again and crossed to the door. "You'd better get dressed," he told her quietly. "Mind if I use the guest-room shower?"

The guest room. So he could keep distance between them. She nodded, accepting his choice. "Go right ahead. Your things are already in there."

She bit her lower lip as she heard the door open and then close. Behind him.

When Chad came down to the kitchen, Veronica was already there, dressed and ready to face a day that had everything riding on it.

Angela glanced up at him the moment he crossed the threshold. She looked disgusted, and for a moment he thought that perhaps the woman had somehow divined the connection he and Veronica had made during the long night.

But Angela merely gestured at the table with its offerings.

''Maybe you can make her eat,'' she declared. ''She's not touching anything again.''

''Have the juice.'' There was no nonsense in his voice as he pushed the glass in front of Veronica. ''I can't have you light-headed.''

Her emotions in a jumble, Veronica sat contemplating the full glass for a moment, then picked it up and forced the juice down. He was right. She needed something in her system. She felt her stomach tighten in anticipation as the juice went down.

A little like her last night, she thought. But that was last night and today was today.

He watched her out of the corner of his eye as he jotted down notes to himself. ''Now the toast.'' He pushed another plate toward her.

Veronica made no effort to pick up a piece. ''Quit while you're ahead.''

His eyes met hers. ''I intend to.'' He glanced toward her plate. ''But not about this.''

Because Angela was there, she wasn't free to say what she wanted to.

''I have to make a couple of calls,'' he told her, taking out his cell phone and slipping off the stool. ''When I get back, I want to see that gone.'' He pointed to her plate, then stepped out into the atrium to make his calls in private.

She stared at him through the glass, then picked up a piece of toast and slowly began to eat.

Chapter 13

Despite the constant drone of noise around her, Veronica could hear the sound of her heels as they made contact with the depot floor. She walked quickly beside Chad, looking about, wondering if the kidnapper was here somewhere, watching her.

She saw a child and her heart stopped. But it wasn't Casey. It was someone else's child, tugging on his mother's hand. A sense of longing mixed with envy filled her.

Was he here yet? Was her son here somewhere, being held on to by the man who had kidnapped him?

The pounding in her head increased as she scanned the area.

The Amtrak station still had the pristine feel to

it that new buildings had. Given the number of
commuters milling around, it seemed like an incredible feat. What struck her most was the bright-
ness of the place. There were no sinister shadows
where a kidnapper could be lurking, no dark, un-
derground tunnels where he could quickly escape,
eluding them. Everything was out in the open, il-
luminated either by the sun pouring in through an
immense skylight or the panels of fluorescent lights
artfully placed around the large facility. It would
have been a place she'd have picked for the
exchange. That the kidnapper had selected it made
her wonder.

And gave her hope.

The lockers were near the far entrance. The second she saw them, Veronica hooked her arm
through Chad's and pulled him over.

"I see them," he told her needlessly. The number the kidnapper had specified was located exactly
in the middle, as if to taunt them. "The good thing
about it," Chad told her as they reached the lockers,
"is that there's no way anyone can come and take
the briefcase out without our seeing them. Got the
key?"

Veronica handed it to him and he inserted it into
the lock. It fit. "But what if we miss him somehow?"

Chad opened the door. "There's no way we
could all miss him."

"All?"

He'd taken care of matters while she was getting

ready—while trying to erase images of her and last night from his head. He'd been far more successful with the former than the latter.

"I've got people planted here." He gave her a reassuring look before lifting the briefcase and placing it into the double locker. "The agency doesn't like leaving things to chance—or taking the word of a kidnapper."

So there were other people on their side here. Could she pick them out? Veronica scanned the immediate vicinity a second time with no more enlightenment than the first time. Everyone looked innocent. Everyone looked like a suspect.

Chad closed the door and turned the key, then returned it to Veronica. "Now we wait."

Veronica stared at the locker. So near and yet so far. She didn't know if she could take much more. "We wait," she repeated.

They were early. He had to get her mind occupied somehow. Chad glanced over his shoulder. There was a small coffee shop next to a magazine stand.

There were tables for two scattered in front of the shop. Sitting there, they'd have a clear view of the locker—and anyone who came by to open it. There was no point in hiding. The kidnapper had said that Casey would be brought to the station and released once the money was secure.

Everything that had ever gone into making him a good cop told him this was far too easy.

Taking her arm, Chad indicated the tables.

"Want some coffee?" She began to shake her head. "Casey'll be able to see you from over there," he pointed out.

She blinked as the words penetrated. "Sure. Coffee."

The thought of coffee made her stomach lurch, but holding the cup would give her something to do, and it was an excuse to sit at a table.

Where Casey could see her. She held on to the thought like a good-luck charm.

"I'll be right back," Chad promised, giving her arm a squeeze. "Get a table."

She nodded, moving like a zombie. Her eyes never left the lockers. That the other tables were empty, save for one occupant, registered only peripherally. She took a seat at a table that could be judged to be an inch or two closer to the bank of lockers than the others.

Chad emerged from the shop less than five minutes later, holding two large containers of coffee and balancing a glazed confection of some sort that almost slid off the plate as he set it down.

"For energy," he told her, though she hadn't asked. "Take a piece."

"Maybe later."

Her fingers were cold as he pushed the coffee toward her. Chad covered her hand with his.

She raised her eyes to his, seeking strength. He seemed so calm, so in control, while she felt as if she was going to fall to pieces again. How many times would she coast down this slope before the ordeal was finally over? *Would* it ever be over? The past couple of days had felt like an eternity.

"Do you think he'll really come?"

That part seemed straightforward enough. The tricky part was going to be catching their man. "He will if he wants the money." He felt her fingers curl into her hand beneath his. Chad had no doubt she was digging her nails in. "I won't insult you by telling you to relax, but maybe you should try to breathe a bit more deeply and evenly."

The suggestion brought a silent smile to her lips, which was all that he'd been after. Settling back to wait, Chad stretched out his legs, seeming not to have a care in the world. But one look into his eyes said otherwise.

He brought the cup to his lips, his eyes never straying from his target.

The exchange was to have been made at noon. The minutes dragged by, even as people hurried by them in both directions. The only time Veronica moved was to shift for a better view of the locker when someone momentarily blocked it.

People had come and gone within the busy station, but not a single one had approached the locker with the money in it. The knot in her stomach tightened.

By twelve-fifty she knew something had gone horribly wrong.

For the first time she spared a look at Chad. "Maybe he's changed his mind." The words, the insecurities began to tumble out faster and faster. "Maybe he's afraid to come because he thinks we've set a trap." A worse possibility occurred to her. "Or maybe something's happened to him and Casey."

Unable to stand the direction her thoughts were taking, Veronica covered her mouth with her hands to keep the wave of hysteria back. She couldn't fall apart now, she couldn't.

"Stop it." A vein of kindness ran beneath the gruff command. Veronica looked at him again, dropping her hands to her lap. "You'll make yourself crazy."

But he couldn't dispute that something was definitely not right. It hadn't felt right since one minute after twelve. Maybe before. Though he had watched the locker the entire time and knew that Rusty and Sam were covering both ends of the terminal, Chad couldn't shake the nagging feeling that something had gone awry. The kidnapper hadn't shown up, but he didn't think it was for any of the reasons Veronica had come up with.

Instinct told him that the kidnapper wouldn't just walk away from the money.

He rose to his feet. Veronica stared at him. "Where are you going?"

"To check out a hunch." He crossed quickly to the bank of lockers with Veronica hurrying beside him.

"What kind of hunch?"

He didn't answer. Instead, he asked her for the key.

"Why? No one opened the locker. I was watching the whole time." But she handed it to him.

"So was I, but I just want to make sure." He opened the door. And found the locker completely empty. Part of him had been expecting it, yet it seemed impossible. "How the hell…?"

Veronica moved him aside to look for herself. There was nothing to see.

"Where is it?" she demanded. Frustration and confusion rang in her voice. She'd been watching the entire time. How had anyone gotten past her? "I didn't see anyone open it." She looked at Chad. "Did you?"

"No." Taking out his cell phone, Chad pressed the single number that got him in touch with both men in the terminal. "The money's gone."

Within seconds Rusty and Sam converged from opposite ends of the station. One look at their stunned expressions told Chad that neither of them had seen anyone approach the lockers, either.

Chad stared into the lockers. "Damn it, the guy's not a magician. The briefcase can't just disappear. Where is it?" As he began to swing the door closed in disgust, throwing the empty locker into darkness, something caught his eye. There was a pinprick of light squeezing in at the rear base of the locker. He looked at Sam. "What's behind this locker?"

"Another bank of lockers," Sam told him.

The answer was so simple he could have kicked

himself. He'd seen the other wall of lockers when he'd first walked in.

Silently calling himself an idiot, Chad hurried around to the other side. The door of the locker behind the one they'd been watching wasn't completely closed. As if someone had pushed it into place but hadn't bothered to make sure it had closed all the way. At first glance, it appeared to be identical to the one that had contained the briefcase.

"Just another empty locker," Rusty told his brother.

"You still have that Swiss Army knife I gave you for your twelfth birthday?" Chad asked. The beaten-up knife, which Chad had found, had been one of Rusty's prized possessions when he'd been growing up.

Rusty dug into his pocket. "Never without it." He handed it to Chad.

Quickly Chad ran the length of it along the back wall. The barrier gave way. Chad swore, closing the knife. "Every magic trick has a secret. We were all watching the front because that's where he told us to watch. Nobody bothered watching the other set of lockers. The kidnapper must have gotten in here earlier, rented this locker and weakened the wall just enough to be able to remove it and grab the briefcase. Perfect setup."

He was explaining the mechanics, only Veronica didn't care about the mechanics. She wanted her son. "But where's Casey? Oh, God, Chad, where's Casey?"

As if in response, Chad's cell phone rang.

He pulled it out immediately, not sure what to expect or hope for. The caller could even be the kidnapper. The man was certainly resourceful enough. "Maybe we'll find out now."

But instead of a tinny sound, it was Megan's voice on the other end of the line. "Chad, I just intercepted a 911 call on Ben's shortwave."

Megan wouldn't be telling him this if it wasn't somehow related to the case. Chad purposely avoided looking at Veronica. "About?"

"The call came in from Neil Reinholt's apartment. He's been shot. I know he's on your suspect list, so I went there and arrived just as the paramedics were taking him to the hospital. He was barely conscious, but he was trying to get someone to listen to him. I heard him say 'Casey,' but he lost consciousness before he could say anything more. It could be he was worried about the boy, but I think it was something more."

"Damn." Had someone wanted Neil out of the way? Or had it just been one of his shady creditors out for blood?

Veronica felt as if she was going to leap out of her skin at any second. Hearing Chad swear sent her over the edge. "What is it? Chad, tell me. What is it? Is it about Casey?"

"I'm not sure"

He was about to break the connection when his sister called, "Chad, wait!"

"Neil's been shot," he told Veronica as he brought the phone to his ear again. "Hello?"

"There might be more. I don't know if this is anything, but you know Neil's girlfriend, Josephine?"

Those hairs were standing up at the back of his neck again. "What about her?"

"Savannah tried cross-referencing everything she could think of this morning, and she came across something really odd. Josephine's last name is Sharpe. So is Anne Sullivan's maiden name. There might be a connection. Oh, and one more thing. Rusty sent your tape out to the lab for a final breakdown early this morning. That voice on the tape belongs to a woman."

Bingo. "Thanks, Megan. You've been a great help." He flipped the cell phone closed.

Veronica grabbed his arm, determined to get his attention. "What *is* it?"

"Our kidnapper's a woman." He looked at Rusty. "Megan said the lab results came in." His hand to the small of her back, Chad began to usher Veronica out of the terminal. "I'll fill you in on the way." He glanced over his shoulder at his brother and Sam as he left. "Thanks for your help, anyway."

"On the way to where?" Veronica asked as they hurried through the parking lot to Chad's car. "Do you know where Casey is?"

"No," he answered, "but I think I know someone who might." He opened his door and got in.

Veronica slid in on her side. "We're going to Anne Sullivan's house."

The seat belt slipped from her fingers, and she grabbed for it. "Anne? But we've already talked to her about the caterers." This wasn't about the caterers, she realized. This was something a great deal darker. "What does Anne have to do with Casey's kidnapping?"

It hurt him to break apart the few illusions she had allowed herself, and he didn't even understand why it hurt. He just knew it did. "Maybe everything." He glanced at her quickly, trying to read her expression. She looked numb. "Did you know that her maiden name's the same as Neil's girlfriend's?"

"No. I told you, Neil never told me Josephine's last name, and I didn't bother..." The mention of her brother-in-law reminded her of what else she'd heard. "Chad, you said Neil was shot."

"He was." Her pale complexion turned almost alabaster. "That was Megan calling from his apartment. There's a police-band radio in the office. She heard a 911 call come in from Neil. No details. She recognized the name and took off. Someone apparently shot your brother-in-law. Megan said the only thing she heard him say was your son's name."

She didn't want to believe it. How could Neil be involved? He loved Casey. There had to be some mistake. Afraid that there wasn't, Veronica covered her face with her hands, praying for strength, pray-

ing for her son, and most of all, praying they would
be in time to save him.

She wasn't saying anything. Concerned, Chad allowed himself another glance in her direction before looking back at the road. One o'clock was still
lunchtime, and the streets were crowded with people hurrying to squeeze in a day's worth of errands
into an hour or less. "Are you all right?"

She emerged from behind her hands, her expression stony as she struggled to reconcile what he'd
told her with what, until a few moments ago she'd
felt she knew.

"No, I'm not all right. But I will be the minute
we get Casey back." Determined, she sat up, leaning forward as if that could somehow add to the
momentum and get them to Anne's house faster.
"Step on it."

He didn't point out that they were already weaving in and out of traffic, flying across intersections
whose lights had turned amber and were about to
blush into red. "Consider it stepped on."

The speedometer strained forward as he kept an
eye out for other speeding vehicles that could im-
pede them—and for the police. The latter would
only be a plus. They could use police backup right
about now.

It was beginning to fit together, albeit with gaps.
He'd been right all along about Casey knowing his
kidnapper. They'd just been looking at the wrong
gender. "When you saw that photograph of Casey,
you said he looked happy."

It took Veronica a second to focus, and then she nodded. "He did. I thought...I was hoping that the kidnapper told him they were playing a game."

"Maybe," he allowed. "And maybe the reason Casey looked unafraid was because he knew his kidnapper."

"You mean Neil."

"Neil figures into it somehow," Chad replied, "but Megan said it was a woman's voice on the tape. That doesn't make any sense if Neil was behind the kidnapping scheme." He didn't care for the man, but Veronica's brother-in-law had seemed genuinely surprised when she had told him Casey had been kidnapped. The man just didn't strike him as that good an actor.

He was thinking out loud. The more he talked, the more things continued to drift into place.

"When you went to pick Casey up from the party and found he wasn't there, did you try looking around for him?"

"I was going to, but then the kidnapper called, asking for me."

Just before she was going to start looking, Chad thought. Which could mean that the kidnapper was watching her the entire time. That placed Casey's kidnapper somewhere on the property.

Chad hadn't had a very good look at the Sullivan place. He should have. "If you had looked for him," Chad pressed, "where would you have looked?"

She tried to think. "Andy's room, I suppose. The

grounds—most of the party was held outdoors.'' She closed her eyes for a moment, trying to visualize the premises. ''Maybe the guest house.''

The light was red a full second before he reached the intersection. Chad stepped down hard on the brake. The car fishtailed before stopping. He looked at her. ''The guest house?'' He didn't remember noticing one.

''Way in the back,'' she told him. ''It's little more than a pool house, really. Anne had it converted about a year ago. Casey loved hanging around the construction site. He said it was a house just his size.'' A light dawned. ''Oh, God, you don't think he was there all the time, do you? But he couldn't have been. I was with Anne when the kidnapper phoned. She couldn't have been the one who made the call.''

The light changed and he hit the gas. A sense of urgency refused to release him. ''She's not in this alone.'' The woman was far too high-strung to have done this on her own. ''She had a partner. Someone who could keep Casey occupied.'' He looked at her as they took a sharp turn. ''Someone like Neil's latest girlfriend.''

The voice on the machine had been distorted. She had naturally thought it was a man. The possibility that it had been a woman had just never occurred to her. Now that they knew it was, the thought filled her with horror and revulsion. ''Neil said Josephine played in a band. He bragged that she was an expert with audio equipment. I thought he meant in setting up the speakers."

"Don't blame yourself. These days, almost any amateur could distort their voice. All it takes is a little software, a synthesizer and a computer."

It was all so clear to her now. "Neil came by a couple of times to take him to the ballpark, and she was with him. Casey likes her—" she cried.

"He'll grow up to have better taste," Chad assured her. *If we get to him in time.*

He had the uneasy feeling that the money had been taken without exchanging it for the boy for a reason. Casey could identify his kidnappers. Which meant he was a liability and had to be disposed of.

Chad felt his blood run cold as he pressed the gas pedal harder.

"Can't this car go any faster?"

"Not unless we're willing to cause a major accident." He pulled out his phone again, hitting Rusty's number.

"Rusty, I need you to get to Josephine Sharpe's apartment. If she's there, hold her any way you can. Savannah's got the address for you. I'm on my way to Anne Sullivan's house. Nearly there, in fact." He glanced at Veronica's face, conveying encouragement as best he could. "I think between the two of us, we might be able to wind this up today."

"You got it, Chad."

Chad dropped the cell phone onto his lap as the connection ended, grabbing the wheel with both hands and swerving to the left to avoid being hit by the car that was barreling down Anne Sullivan's driveway.

A small blond child twisted around in the back seat and waved gaily at Veronica.

Chapter 14

"**O**migod, that's Casey!" Veronica cried. She rose in her seat as if to leap out of the car.

"Hang on," Chad warned.

He swung the wheel all the way to the right, turning his car a full 180 degrees. Tires screeched and the brakes groaned in protest as he brought the car forward again. Pressing down hard on the gas pedal again, he began to chase the maroon Mercedes. The other car had already made it down the winding hill and was flying into the main flow of traffic. Cars swerved right and left to avoid a collision.

Veronica watched in horror as Anne's car careened in and out of traffic. "She's going to get him killed. Do something!" she begged.

"Call Ben for me on your phone," he ordered.

Chad couldn't risk taking his eyes off the road to make the call himself. Swerving to avoid the nose of a Honda that had just swerved to get out of the Mercedes's way, Chad rattled off the phone number to Veronica.

Frantically pawing through her purse, she located her phone. The numbers danced through her head. "What is it again?" Chad repeated Ben's number and she punched it in. A sound finally buzzed against her ear as she prayed. "It's ringing." Veronica thrust the cell phone into his hand.

"Hello, Ben? Chad. I'm traveling south on Deerfield, just passed MacArthur, and I've got the kidnapper's car in my sights. Maroon Mercedes, California plates." He recited the numbers he could no longer see but had committed to memory. "I think she might be on her way to the airport. I need squad cars as fast as possible."

"You're sure it's the kidnapper?" Ben asked.

Chad had seen Veronica's stricken face when she'd recognized Casey. "The boy's in the back seat. I'm sure."

"I'm on it." Ben didn't even bother signing off

Every second counted. Chad knew Ben was already calling the plate numbers in to one of his friends on the force. Now all they needed was luck. A lot of it.

He could feel Veronica's disbelief being eaten away by tension.

She was hardly aware of taking the cell phone

back from him. "Anne was in the driver's seat, wasn't she?"

"It might have been. The woman had auburn hair, but I didn't get a good look at her." He'd been too busy trying to get out of the way. "Could have been Josephine." Now that he thought of it, their hair color was similar.

It seemed incredible, yet she'd seen Casey in the car with her own eyes. A brief glimpse was all she'd gotten, but there was no mistaking that grin. It was her son. "How could Anne have done something so awful? Our kids are best friends. *We've* been close friends for ten years."

"Obviously not as close as you thought."

He was going more than fifteen miles over the speed limit, and the kidnapper was still getting away. Thoughts of cars crashing into one another in his wake had Chad's adrenaline pumping to new heights.

The distant sound of sirens became audible. The cavalry was coming, he thought, relieved.

Veronica was leaning forward, straining against her seat belt, her fingers digging into the dashboard. She gasped as the Mercedes narrowly avoided crashing into a city bus.

"Is Anne capable of doing something desperate?" he asked her.

Her mouth twisted in a half smile at the irony of the question. "You mean, other than kidnapping my son?"

"Point taken." Chad left it up to her to answer or not.

"I don't know." She never took her eyes off the maroon car, scarcely breathing. It felt as if her heart was lodged in her throat. "I didn't think she was capable of doing anything desperate at all. Until now." Afraid, Veronica turned her gaze to Chad. "Why?"

"Because we're closing in on her, and unless my hearing's off, so are about three squad cars."

The Mercedes was driving erratically, abruptly turning into the parking lot of a small shopping mall. People scattered right and left as the driver tried desperately to elude pursuers and get away.

Suddenly a squad car pulled up directly in front of the Mercedes, turning so that its hood faced the fleeing car. Chad slammed on the brakes, stopping directly behind the Mercedes. Between them they cut off any avenue of escape for the Mercedes. Two more squad cars pulled up on either side of it. Policemen poured out of all three vehicles, their service revolvers drawn and trained on the occupants of the Mercedes.

Chad leaped out of his car. Veronica was less than a heartbeat behind him.

"There's a child in there!" he shouted, waving his arms over his head to get the policemen's attention. Out of the corner of his eye, he recognized Ben's car pulling up in the distance. Reinforcements.

Warily the policemen lowered their weapons, but left them unholstered.

Unable to wait a single second longer, ignoring the guns, Veronica ducked around Chad to reach the Mercedes rear door. She yanked it open just as Anne was emerging from the driver's seat, sobbing, her hands shaking as she raised them in the air.

"Mommy, where have you been?" Casey exclaimed, his voice echoing with curiosity and pleasure as he wrapped his arms tightly around her. "I've missed you."

She tried very hard not to cry as she held him close. She was failing miserably. "And I've missed you." Pressing the boy to her heart, she rose to her feet again, thinking she was never going to let him out of her arms again.

Tears blinding her, she looked for Chad.

"Mommy, you're squashing me," Casey protested.

"Sorry," she murmured, kissing the top of his head.

Anne stood blocking the driver's side, her arms over her head. "Please, please, don't shoot. My son's in the car. Don't shoot," she begged.

Gabriel Saldana moved ahead of the other policemen, taking charge. "Ben filled me in," he informed Chad, recognizing him from Ben's description. Taking cuffs out, he gently but firmly turned Anne around and took hold of her wrist. "Anne Sullivan, you're under arrest for the kidnapping of

Casey Reinholt. You have the right to remain silent…"

He never got a chance to put on the second handcuff. Anne gave a little moan and fainted.

Managing to catch her before she hit the ground, Gabriel shook his head. "First time I've had a suspect faint on me."

Andy wriggled out of the car, running to Anne, fear and confusion on his small face. "Mommy, Mommy, get up!" He began to tug on her shoulder "Please get up."

Still holding Casey, Veronica shifted him so that he rested on her hip. Supporting him with one hand, she extended the other to Andy, smiling encouragingly at the boy. "You're going to come home with me for a while, Andy."

Overhearing, Chad looked at her. He would have thought she'd want to distance herself from anything that had to do with the kidnapping and Anne. She was an endless source of amazement to him.

"Is the game over, Mommy?" Casey wanted to know.

She pressed another kiss to his hair, her heart quickening when she thought of how close she'd come to losing him. "Yes, baby, the game's over."

"Mom, don't call me baby," he said in what he thought was a whisper. He jerked his head toward his friend, who was now clutching Veronica's free hand. "Andy'll hear you."

"Sorry, I forgot." A quirky smile played along

her lips. He was still her normal little boy. She was one of the lucky ones.

She turned to look at Chad, tears welling up in her eyes for the second time in as many minutes. There were absolutely no words she could say to thank him, to thank any of them, for what they had done.

For a second Chad let himself go and put his arm around her shoulders. "You're crying again."

She sniffed, a smile breaking through even though tears were sliding down her cheeks. "Good tears."

"Oh." As if he understood the difference.

Digging into his pocket, Chad fished out a handkerchief that was badly wrinkled, but clean. He offered it to her, then realized she didn't have a hand available. Chad started to say something to Andy, then thought better of it. Instead, he wiped away the tears himself. Something nameless, but no less unsettling for its anonymity, stirred within him as she looked up at him. Clearing his throat, he pocketed the handkerchief and walked toward the lead squad car.

Just now coming to, Anne had been placed in the squad car's back seat, her hands cuffed behind her. Hurrying by Chad, Gabriel rounded the hood, then stopped for a second to look at the Mercedes. He gave a low whistle of appreciation. He looked at Chad.

"That baby's no more than six weeks old by my

estimation. What's a woman with that kind of money doing kidnapping her best friend's kid?''

"That's what I'd like to find out. Mind if I tag along to the station?'' Chad took out his wallet, showing Gabriel his identification by way of supporting his request. "Got a few people on the LAPD who will vouch for me.'' Ben finally managed to reach them. The crowd around them had gathered quickly and was six deep in places. "Including Ben,'' Chad added, nodding at the man.

"Good enough for me,'' Gabriel told him, getting into the squad car. "Just as long as you don't get in the way.''

"Thanks.'' Chad glanced in Veronica's direction. She was unfinished business. "I'll follow in my car,'' he said, stepping back. He turned toward Veronica.

"Is Anne all right?'' she asked, nodding at the unconscious woman in the back seat.

"She just fainted. I think everything finally sank in.'' He motioned for Ben to come forward. "Ben'll take you and the boys home in his car. I'll be by as soon as I learn anything,'' he promised.

"All right.'' About to leave with Ben, she stopped to kiss Chad, catching him completely by surprise. Her eyes held his for a moment. "Thank you.''

A warm spot opened up in his chest. He ignored it, or tried to, and dismissed her words with a shrug. "Just doing my job.''

He stood a moment longer, watching her walk

off with the children. Trying to get his bearings. They kept eluding him.

He'd come to the realization that Veronica was full of surprises. So when she turned up half an hour later in the hallway of the Bedford police station, outside one of the rooms reserved for interrogation, Chad wasn't entirely caught off guard.

Still, there were other places he had expected to see her first.

"What are you doing here?" He looked directly behind her, expecting to see a small entourage. "Where are the boys?"

"I left Casey and Andy with Angela. She was overjoyed to see Casey. Andy's a little shaken up, but Casey seems fine." She smiled. Casey was more than fine. He was his old self, playful and incredibly thoughtful for a boy his age. "He's trying to distract Andy with the latest video game."

He'd thought that perhaps she'd come here with some earth-shattering revelation that Casey had confided to her on the way home. Since the boy obviously hadn't, it brought Chad back to his original question.

"You could have told me all that when I came over." He looked into her eyes. "What are you doing here?"

She'd persuaded the sergeant at the front desk to bring her back here after explaining who she was. Chad was going to need more of an explanation than that. Veronica looked at the closed door directly behind him and wondered if that was where they were holding Anne.

"I want to know why." She looked at Chad meaningfully. "And I think that Anne is going to need someone in her corner."

"In her corner?" He stared at her. The woman shook up everything he thought he knew about the human race. He knew the full story behind the kidnapping now. Once she had come to, Anne had been more than willing to give the police a full confession, waiving her right to a lawyer. To the charitable mind, there were explanations and extenuating circumstances for what she had done, but none that Veronica was familiar with yet. Which made her reason for being here so hard to understand. "How can you be in her corner? The woman kidnapped your son and put you through hell."

"I know." None of this made any sense to her, but she knew, at the bottom of her heart, what she was feeling. Despite everything, she felt compassion. "But something had to have gone horribly wrong for Anne. She wouldn't have done this terrible thing unless something forced her to do it. I need to understand what that was."

And with understanding came forgiveness. He knew that was what she was thinking. He was beginning to know her far better than he thought was safe.

"What are you—a saint?" The question had come out sarcastically, but he didn't attempt to temper it. She needed to be shaken up a little so that she could see the world for what it was. People fell into bad situations all the time, had their backs against the wall with nowhere to turn, but they didn't resort to kidnapping.

She sighed, not wanting to argue with him. He was the one who'd saved her son. And her soul. "No, not a saint, just human. I have my son back and he's not harmed. That's all that matters."

Hearts like hers left themselves open to being hurt—didn't she understand that? Anne might not have been the mastermind of the plot, but she had been a key player. "Well, he came damn close to being hurt. You realize that, don't you?"

Veronica said nothing for a moment, trying to come to terms with the fear that suddenly spiked through her. She knew it would be a long time before she could finally bury it. But to be able to do that, she needed to know all the details once and for all. Now, with no surprises later.

"Tell me," she said. "All of it. Everything you know." She gave him a starting point. Ben had told her what hospital Neil had been taken to, and she'd called to find out his condition. The nurse had said he was stable. "What does my brother-in-law have to do with it?"

"Other than bringing the viper into the fold, very little. Not that he had much of a chance of saying no. Josephine made sure she was in the right place at the right time, with all the right words to stroke his ego." The police had brought her in a short while ago, screaming obscenities at anyone within earshot. "From what I gather, Josephine's the mastermind behind all this. They just brought her in." He nodded at another room down at the far end of the hall. "But she's lawyered up. Not that it matters that much." Not with Anne giving a sworn statement. The jury would believe a socialite before they'd believe the story of a ragtag guitarist of a third-rate band.

Despite herself, Veronica shivered. She ran her hands along her arms. "Was she the one who shot Neil?"

"Yes, she was." Chad took off his jacket and draped it over her shoulders.

"No, it's all right," she began to protest.

"Keep it on." It was an order, not subject to debate. "Neil overheard Josephine on the phone with Anne and pieced things together. Apparently he had *some* scruples, and he told her he was going to call the police. That was when she shot him. She told Anne she killed him—I guess you socialite types are stronger than you look. Josephine was coming to get Casey."

She didn't want to let her mind go there, but she couldn't help it. "But not to bring him to me." It wasn't really a question.

"No, not to bring him to you," he agreed slowly. "Casey could identify both of them, and Josephine was not about to spend her new fortune in prison. She told Anne to get him ready. Anne was afraid that Josephine was going to kill him, too, so she took the boys and started to run. That's when we caught up to her.''

He still hadn't answered what she wanted to know. ''But why do this to begin with?''

''For the oldest reason in the world. Money. Seems your best friend didn't share everything with you. She was too ashamed.''

Veronica couldn't bring herself to think of Anne as a coldhearted manipulator. ''Of what?''

''Seems that her husband's got a damn good divorce lawyer. He used an earlier indiscretion of hers as leverage and got off without paying alimony, child support or the customary fifty-fifty split because of alienated affections.''

She knew about the so-called indiscretion. ''That happened six years ago when they were separated. He'd almost demolished Anne's self-esteem. When someone started paying attention to her, she was so hungry for affection she made a mistake. But only that one night.''

''Apparently once was all it took.''

That was so unfair. ''But he's the one running off with a woman half his age.''

''According to his lawyer—'' he was quoting Anne, ''—it was after the fact.''

The hell it was. Her heart was going out to Anne more and more by the minute. ''And the child support?''

''Her about-to-be ex claims that Andy's a result of that little liaison your friend had. He says Andy's not his. The upshot is, Anne was desperate. Des-

perate enough to listen to her cousin's plan. At least
at first. To her credit, she says she tried to back out
of it, but Josephine wouldn't let her. She threatened
to go to the police. Anne was afraid of her.''

That Veronica could well understand. There had
been something about the woman's eyes that had
made Veronica uneasy in her presence. ''Josephine's her cousin?''

He nodded. ''According to Anne, they share a
second aunt or something. And now they'll share a
prison cell,'' he said grimly. ''At least figuratively.
I suspect the DA'll be more lenient with Anne because she did try to save your son.'' In his book,
though, she didn't earn many points for that. ''But
the way I see it, if she hadn't provided the opportunity in the first place and then kept him in the
guest house, there would have been no need to save
him, because there would have been no kidnapping.''

Casey had answered her questions on the way
home, but she'd tried not to ask too many, afraid
that she would make him realize that this all hadn't
been a big game the way he'd been told.

''The guest house? Was Casey there all the
time?'' Why hadn't she gone there to look for him?
Why hadn't her mother's instinct told her he was
there?

''All the time.'' He studied her face, trying to
read her thoughts. Her brow was furrowed, and before he could stop himself, he eased the furrows
away with the tips of his fingers. Their eyes held

for a long moment. He talked himself out of kissing her. The case was over and there was no sense making himself suffer over something he'd known from the start wasn't meant to be. "Still want to stand by her?"

It took Veronica a moment to examine her conscience to make certain. Nothing had changed. If anything, her conviction had only grown stronger. "Yes."

He shook his head in disbelief. "After all she's done to you? Damn, Veronica Lancaster, but you are one rare woman."

She didn't see it that way. "There but for the grace of God..."

Who was she kidding? He knew her better than that. "You wouldn't have stolen Andy if the tables had been turned."

"No." She knew that for certain, but who knew what desperate thing she might have been capable of if she had been afraid like Anne. "But then, I've never been tested that way, either." She saw him begin to disagree and placed a finger to his lips, silencing him. "It doesn't matter. We can debate this thing forever. The bottom line is that she did save my son. She didn't let anything happen to him. For three days I've been haunted by the fear that this wasn't going to be resolved in any manner I could live with. But it was." And now that it was, she could get on with her life. "I'm going to call her a lawyer—and not the one she had handling her divorce."

He laughed shortly and folded his arms. She certainly was something else. "I suppose you'll be a character witness, too."

There was no hesitation. "If it helps."

Chad knew there was no way he was going to get her to leave. In her own refined, genteel way, the woman could be as stubborn as the best of them. "C'mon, I'll see if I can get you a few minutes with Anne. As long as you promise not to try to spring her."

She held up her hand, a smile playing on her lips. "You have my word." The dimple in her cheek deepened.

He talked himself out of kissing her again, but it was getting harder.

Chapter 15

Chad brought Veronica home an hour later. He stood back and watched as Casey rushed up to greet her, and listened as she told Andy that his mother sent her love and would be with him as soon as she could. Listened and marveled at how upbeat Veronica sounded. He'd never met anyone quite like her and knew he probably never would again.

The boys went off to play, and the housekeeper retreated after asking if there was anything special Veronica wanted for dinner. She'd opted for hot dogs and French fries, favorites of both Casey and Andy.

That left the two of them alone.

There was nothing left to do except tie up loose ends. Tie up loose ends while he felt his stomach tie itself in knots he had no idea how to undo. He followed her in silence as she went to the den to write the check that would terminate their association.

He'd known when he took on her case that he had no place in her life. That his only function was to help her, and for that she was paying the same sort of fee all the other clients who'd come to ChildFinders, Inc., had.

Except that he hadn't slept with any of the other clients.

Because she wasn't like any of the others.

But that was his problem to deal with, not hers, and the sooner he came to grips with that, the better for everyone all around. Maybe even him.

Veronica could feel a tension creep in between them and wondered why. She took her checkbook from the center desk drawer she'd unlocked. "Shall I make the check out to you?"

"To the agency will be fine," he told her. Veronica put pen to paper. He felt awkward watching her write out the check for services he'd rendered. Accepting it from her would put the cap on their relationship.

They hadn't had a relationship, he reminded himself tersely. At least, not one that, under normal circumstances, would have evolved. These hadn't been normal circumstances. Suddenly finding herself the mother of a kidnapped child was like finding herself thrown into the middle of a war. Things happened in wartime that didn't take place in everyday life.

Such as feeling he had the right to make love to a woman who had been born to the finer things in life. She needed someone from her own world, he told himself, not a man who was still wrestling with the demons from his past.

As if she would even consider being part of his life or having him be part of hers. The thought mocked him. What happened between them came under the heading of "just one of those things." An interlude, nothing more. If he tried to imbue it with any more importance than that, he was a bigger fool than he'd thought.

It was time to get things back to normal.

Finished, Veronica held the check out to him. "Let me know if this isn't enough."

He glanced at the sum. "You made it out for too much."

But when he tried to give the check back to her, Veronica pushed his hand away with a smile.

"No amount is too much, not for what you did. I was willing to give up every penny I have and beg and borrow more if I needed to." Looking up into his eyes, she folded his fingers over the check. "This doesn't begin to cover it. Consider it a small token of my appreciation."

The thought rankled him more than he knew it should have. Maybe because of the emphasis on their different stations in life. Hers said "blue blood," his said "passing through." "The agreement didn't include 'tokens.'"

Something in his voice made her wary. "Then call it a donation to the agency—to help find other missing children."

He nodded, not willing to continue arguing the point. Drawing his hand away from hers, he pocketed the check. "Thank you. Cade's been talking about getting more state-of-the-art equipment."

Inspiration leaped forward and she reached for her checkbook again. "If he needs a larger donation—"

He cut her off. He didn't want their last words to be about money. "He'll know where to come."

That had come out too curtly, but he didn't want to be reminded of their very different lifestyles. Not right now.

He was sufficiently aware of that as it was.

Chad shoved his hands into his pockets, feeling suddenly uncomfortable in his skin. This was something new, at least with her. But then, reluctance to say goodbye was something new to him, as well.

He looked toward the door. "Unless there's anything more, I'll be going."

Unless there's anything more. The words hovered in the air between them, mocking her.

Wasn't there anything more?

She'd thought there was a great deal more. Veronica looked into his eyes again. Had she only imagined last night? The desire, the passion that had surrounded her so completely? Was that only a figment of her imagination? He'd made love to her in a way she'd never been made love to before. Gently, wildly, and it took her breath away just remembering. After last night—*because* of last night—she'd thought there was more in his heart. That last night hadn't been just about a convenient meeting of bodies.

She'd been the one to ask him to stay, she reminded herself. He hadn't made a single overt move toward her. Maybe he thought she was a frustrated rich widow, throwing herself at him to blot out the hours.

She felt the sting of tears behind her eyes. Could she blame him for thinking that?

But now, apparently, it was over. He had a life to get back to.

And she had Casey.

So why was there this bitter hurt opening up within her? A wound that felt as if it would take a very long time to heal?

She'd never known anyone who hadn't wanted something from her. Even Robert had wanted something. The doors her name had opened up for him.

Chad Andreini wanted nothing from her and she ached because he didn't. Because she wanted so much from him. And she wanted him to want her.

But she had her pride and she wasn't going to ask him to stay. Not a second time. This time the decision had to come from him.

"No," she replied quietly, "there's nothing

more.'' Her throat tightened as she put out her hand. Two strangers about to part.

He took her hand in his, shaking it as if they hadn't spent the night in each other's arms. As if she hadn't been the one to open up the door within him that he'd kept sealed shut for so long.

He nodded toward the ceiling. The boys had gone upstairs to play. ''Say goodbye to Casey for me.''

Veronica set her mouth grimly. ''I will. I guess I'll see you at the trial.''

The trial. He'd almost forgotten about that. He'd be there to testify about what had happened. And she'd be there to testify on behalf of a woman she had every right in the world to hate. A woman who had betrayed her trust and very nearly wrecked her world. That Veronica could be so generous and forgiving still astonished him.

Chad crossed to the doorway. ''Right.''

He walked away without turning around, leaving her standing in the den. He didn't know if he could look at her one last time and still keep walking. So he didn't even try.

She made him want to be a better person.

If Veronica could find it in her heart to forgive Anne Sullivan so quickly even though the woman had been instrumental in kidnapping her son, then maybe, Chad told himself, it was time he let go of the anger he'd been harboring for so long. The anger and the hurt.

The thought lingered on his mind, and he debated

it for the remainder of the day. All through the report he wrote up about the case, all through the conversations he had with the others at the agency, the thought relentlessly haunted him.

Evening found him driving to Harris Memorial Hospital, instead of his empty apartment.

It was time to bury his ghosts and put things right. Way past time.

The hospital parking lot was emptying when he arrived. Most visitors had either gone or were on their way

Chad went to the information desk to ask what room his father was in. A small, grandmotherly woman in a pink smock stopped what she was doing to look it up on the computer. The smile she offered, along with the information, stayed in his mind, reminding him of another, softer smile as he rode the elevator up to the seventh floor.

The floor where they kept the more seriously ill patients.

Chad waited a beat before getting off the elevator, a residue of reluctance slowing him down. He had no idea what he was going to say, only that he needed to say something. For his sake, as well as his father's. He understood that now. This was as much for him as it was for his father.

The man in the single-care unit bed didn't bear any resemblance to the man he had once known. As a child, he'd always thought that his father looked powerful, like a fast-talking wrestling star in his prime. This man before him was old beyond his years, old and tired. The once robust frame had shrunk, pulling into itself. A sadness Chad was unprepared for came over him.

His father stirred, as if sensing his presence. The small, blue eyes opened, squinting as he tried to focus. Jerome Andreini shaded his eyes, though there was little light in the room.

"Chad?" he asked uncertainly, like a man who wasn't sure if he was awake or dreaming.

Chad moved closer to the bed. "I thought I'd stop by and see how you were doing."

His father felt around on the blanket for the control that powered his bed. Seeing it, Chad pushed the small beige rectangle into his father's hand. A grateful smile creased the sunken face. Jerome pressed a button and the top section elevated, allowing him a better view of his son. "I'm doing okay, I guess, for a man with both feet in the grave."

It surprised Chad how much the comment bothered him. "Don't bury yourself yet, old man. While you're lying here counting away your minutes, medicine's making great strides."

The dry laugh ended in a cough. "You didn't used to be an optimist."

He still wasn't. But he was more open to the idea that sometimes things did go right. And open to the idea that sometimes people needed hope, instead of cold, comfortless facts. "Things change."

His father looked at him for a long moment, as if searching for something.

"Yeah," he finally said, "they do." Guilt etched his features. "Look, boy, great medical strides aside, I don't know how much longer I have. I want to tell you… About what happened, I—"

Chad waved his hand, dismissing words that refused to form. "It's in the past. No sense revisiting it, right?"

"Right," his father agreed. "But I still want to say I'm sorry. For everything."

Chad resisted the temptation to say that being sorry didn't change the past. Because it might change the future.

"Okay, you've said it. Now concentrate on getting your strength back." A nurse looked into the room, her manner silently encouraging Chad to take his leave. Visiting hours were over. Relieved, he began edging toward the door. "Well, I'd better be heading out. Like I said, I just wanted to stop by to look in on you."

His father was almost pitifully grateful. "I appreciate it, Chad. I really do."

Maybe he did, Chad thought. Self-conscious, he shrugged away the gratitude. "Let me know if you need anything."

Jerome was all but beaming as he looked at the son he had wronged. The son who had finally forgiven him. "I already got it."

Chad didn't know what to say to that, didn't know how to respond. He mumbled his goodbye and left.

Feeling oddly good for a man who was admittedly pretty miserable.

He couldn't collect his thoughts. They kept drifting away from him like clouds traveling across a clear spring sky, going where he couldn't reach them.

Just like the past few days.

He'd lost track of what day it was. Even the calendar on his desk didn't help. He'd only managed to stare at it blankly.

Hitting the backspace button on his keyboard, he deleted everything he'd attempted to write in the past half hour. A line and a half.

"Want some time off?"

He looked up, surprised to see Cade standing in his doorway. Normally, Chad was keenly aware of his surroundings. Being caught off guard wasn't like him. He was far too preoccupied for his own liking. It had to stop.

But when?

"No," Chad answered, looking back at the blank screen. "Why?"

Cade moved into the room, concerned. "Because you seem a little off your game. You've earned the time, you know, if you want to take it."

Chad began to hunt and peck again, making yet another attempt to write an overdue report on the case that had come before Veronica's. "I don't want to take it," he said curtly. "I just want to go on working."

"It doesn't really work, you know."

Chad looked up. "What doesn't?"

Cade gestured toward the computer and the stack of paper around it. "Trying to bury yourself in work. You've got to come up for air sometime, and that's when it hits you."

He spoke from experience. The agency had been founded because he wanted to find his own missing son, and until that day came, he'd wanted to keep so busy he didn't have time to think. But thoughts came, anyway.

"Whatever it is you're trying to get away from grabs you right by the throat and hangs on." He shook his head at the memory. "I should know."

Chad was well aware of Cade's story, of the years that had gone by before Darin had finally been found. "No offense, but this isn't the same thing."

Cade rested his hip against Chad's desk, his arms folded across his chest. "Oh, I don't know, trying to run from whatever it is that's bothering you is always the same thing. Want my advice?" He didn't wait for Chad to answer. "Deal with it. Or with her."

Chad's back went up instantly. "What makes you think it's a her?"

If Cade had doubted it before, Chad's reaction clinched it. "Because Veronica Lancaster had the same look on her face you do now when she stopped by here yesterday."

"She was here?" What had she been doing here? He thought of Casey. Had someone else taken him?

"She came by to give me a letter of praise to put into your file. I didn't bother telling her I didn't keep files on my partners. The letter's in my office if you want to see it."

Chad shook his head. Seeing it would only prolong a link that was better off broken.

"I got the distinct impression she was hoping to bump into you." Cade began to walk out of Chad's office. "Why don't you see if you can bump into her?"

He made it sound so easy, Chad thought, irritated. "Because she's champagne, and I'm beer."

Cade didn't see it that way, but didn't bother stating it. He went for the obvious. "They can still be served at the same party. And who knows, maybe you can come up with a new drink."

Cade walked out, leaving Chad with something to think about.

If he did any more thinking, his head was going to fall off.

Getting behind the wheel of his car, Chad had every intention of just going home and calling it a day.

But the prospect of facing another night tossing and turning, staring at his ceiling, had him heading his car east, instead of west. Before he could finish calling himself several kinds of fool, he was pulling into her driveway.

The instant he shut off the engine, the front door opened.

He expected to see Angela, but it wasn't the housekeeper who walked out. It was Veronica.

He couldn't read her expression.

For the first time in a week, her heart felt as if it was thawing out. He was here. Finally. "Took your time getting here."

He didn't follow her. "You were expecting me?"

She shook her head as she threaded an arm through his and began to draw him inside. She'd been passing the window when she'd seen his car pull up. It had felt like Christmas. "Not so much expecting as hoping."

Stopping at the front doorstep, he stood his ground, not knowing exactly what that ground was. Only that he needed to be honest with her. "Look, Veronica, I came here because I can't seem to get you out of my mind."

She studied his expression. "You're saying that as if it's a bad thing."

"Well, isn't it?" After all, thinking about her was only driving him crazy.

So was that it? she wondered. Was he trying to get her out of his mind? To forget about her? The thought hurt. "You tell me."

A note of recrimination crept into his voice. "Isn't it wrong to torture yourself, wanting something you know you can't have?"

The wind whipped her hair into her face, and she

pushed it back, never taking her eyes off Chad. "You're making assumptions, aren't you?"

"Assumptions?" He wasn't assuming anything. It was all true.

"About wanting something you can't have." She saw she wasn't getting through to him. For a smart man, he could be awfully dense. "Who said anything about 'can't?' I don't recall any offers being turned down." She looked at him significantly. "Or being made."

"They weren't made because they'd be turned down." Wouldn't they? he began to wonder. No, he was just setting himself up to be disappointed. Guys like him didn't get to live happily ever after with the woman of their choice. Not when that woman was born with a silver spoon in her mouth.

She didn't know whether to hug him or kick him. "Just because you're my hero doesn't give you the right to play God."

"God?"

"God," she repeated, then added, "All knowing—because you're not. You just proved it."

Was she saying what he thought she was saying? It seemed too incredible. And yet… "So if I asked if I could come by sometime, you'd say yes?"

"Yes." The word burst through the sudden bright smile on her lips.

Refusing to allow himself to get carried away, he proceeded slowly. But hope began to build in the hollow spot in his chest. "And if I said I wanted to make love with you again…"

Her eyes were bright. "Yes, again."

He went for broke. "And if I told you I wanted to spend the rest of my life with you..."

Unable to hold back any longer, Veronica threw her arms around his neck. "Yes, oh, yes!"

His arms closed around her. She felt so good like this. "Do you know what you're getting into?"

"Yes." Her eyes spoke volumes as she looked up at him. And suddenly he understood. "Into a relationship with a man I not only respect, but lo—"

Chad pressed his finger to her lips, silencing her. She looked at him, confused. "I get to say it first."

"'It'?" she teased as a lighthearted feeling slipped over her.

"It," he echoed. "The L-word." He grew serious. More serious than he had ever been. "I love you, Veronica. I didn't know what loving someone was until I met you. It's this incredible ache you want to nurture because it makes you feel more alive than you've ever felt before. I stayed away because I didn't think I had a prayer of your feeling the same for me."

She could only smile at him as she shook her head. "I guess that means you're not the perfect investigator, after all. Because I do."

A warmth surged through him. He indicated her front door. "Want to go inside? It's chilly out here for you."

She didn't feel cold at all, not anymore. "That

all depends on which side of your arms I'm standing on.''

He tightened his arms around her. ''The right
side. Finally, the right side.''

She couldn't argue with that. Especially not
when her mouth was otherwise occupied.

It didn't feel cold anymore.

*   *   *   *   *

Look for
AN UNCOMMON HERO,
the next installment in
Marie Ferrarella's popular miniseries,
CHILDFINDERS, INC.,
available in January 2001
from Silhouette Books.

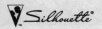

▼ *Silhouette®* —

where love comes alive—online...

eHARLEQUIN.com

your romantic escapes

●—Indulgences
♥ Monthly guides to indulging yourself,
such as:
★ Tub Time: A guide for bathing beauties
★ Magic Massages: A treat for tired feet

●—Horoscopes
♥ Find your daily Passionscope, weekly
Lovescopes and Erotiscopes

♥ Try our compatibility game

●—Reel Love
♥ Read all the latest romantic
movie reviews

●—Royal Romance
♥ Get the latest scoop on your favorite
royal romances

●—Romantic Travel
♥ For the most romantic destinations, hotels
and travel activities

SINTE1

You're not going to believe this offer!

In October and November 2000, buy any two Harlequin or Silhouette books and save $10.00 off future purchases, or buy any three and save $20.00 off future purchases!

Just fill out this form and attach 2 proofs of purchase (cash register receipts) from October and November 2000 books and Harlequin will send you a coupon booklet worth a total savings of $10.00 off future purchases of Harlequin and Silhouette books in 2001. Send us 3 proofs of purchase and we will send you a coupon booklet worth a total savings of $20.00 off future purchases.

Saving money has never been this easy.

I accept your offer! Please send me a coupon booklet:

Name: _____

Address: _____ City: _____

State/Prov.: _____ Zip/Postal Code: _____

Optional Survey!

In a typical month, how many Harlequin or Silhouette books would you buy <u>new</u> at retail stores?

☐ Less than 1   ☐ 1   ☐ 2   ☐ 3 to 4   ☐ 5+

Which of the following statements best describes how you <u>buy</u> Harlequin or Silhouette books? Choose one answer only that <u>best</u> describes you.

☐ I am a regular buyer and reader
☐ I am a regular reader but buy only occasionally
☐ I only buy and read for specific times of the year, e.g. vacations
☐ I subscribe through Reader Service but also buy at retail stores
☐ I mainly borrow and buy only occasionally
☐ I am an occasional buyer and reader

Which of the following statements best describes how you <u>choose</u> the Harlequin and Silhouette series books you buy <u>new</u> at retail stores? By "series," we mean books within a particular line, such as *Harlequin PRESENTS* or *Silhouette SPECIAL EDITION*. Choose one answer only that <u>best</u> describes you.

☐ I only buy books from my favorite series
☐ I generally buy books from my favorite series but also buy books from other series on occasion
☐ I buy some books from my favorite series but also buy from many other series regularly
☐ I buy all types of books depending on my mood and what I find interesting and have no favorite series

Please send this form, along with your cash register receipts as proofs of purchase, to:
In the U.S.: Harlequin Books, P.O. Box 9057, Buffalo, NY 14269
In Canada: Harlequin Books, P.O. Box 622, Fort Erie, Ontario L2A 5X3
(Allow 4-6 weeks for delivery) Offer expires December 31, 2000.

PHQ4002

USA Today Bestselling Author

SHARON SALA

has won readers' hearts with thrilling tales
of romantic suspense. Now Silhouette Books
is proud to present five passionate stories from
this beloved author.

Available in August 2000:
ALWAYS A LADY
A beauty queen whose dreams have been dashed in a
tragic twist of fate seeks shelter for her wounded spirit
in the arms of a rough-edged cowboy....

Available in September 2000:
GENTLE PERSUASION
A brooding detective risks everything to protect the
woman he once let walk away from him....

Available in October 2000:
SARA'S ANGEL
A woman on the run searches desperately for a reclusive
Native American secret agent—the only man who can save
her from the danger that stalks her!

Available in November 2000:
HONOR'S PROMISE
A struggling waitress discovers she is really a rich heiress—
and must enter a powerful new world of wealth and
privilege on the arm of a handsome stranger....

Available in December 2000:
KING'S RANSOM
A lone woman returns home to the ranch where she was
raised, and discovers danger—as well as the man she once
loved with all her heart....

Silhouette invites you to come back to Whitehorn, Montana...

MONTANA MAVERICKS

WED IN WHITEHORN—
12 BRAND-NEW stories that capture living and loving beneath the Big Sky where legends live on and love lasts forever!

M·M

And the adventure continues...

October 2000—
Marilyn Pappano *Big Sky Lawman* (#5)

November 2000—
Pat Warren *The Baby Quest* (#6)

December 2000—
Karen Hughes *It Happened One Wedding Night* (#7)

January 2001—
Pamela Toth *The Birth Mother* (#8)

More MONTANA MAVERICKS coming soon!

Available at your favorite retail outlet.

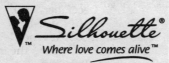

Silhouette®

Where love comes alive™